JAMES BALDWIN
Nobody Knows My Name

James Baldwin was born in 1924 and educated in New York. He is the author of more than twenty works of fiction and nonfiction, including *Go Tell It on the Mountain*, *Notes of a Native Son*, *Giovanni's Room*, *Nobody Knows My Name*, *Another Country*, *The Fire Next Time*, *Nothing Personal*, *Blues for Mister Charlie*, *Going to Meet the Man*, *The Amen Corner*, *Tell Me How Long the Train's Been Gone*, *One Day When I Was Lost*, *No Name in the Street*, *If Beale Street Could Talk*, *The Devil Finds Work*, *Little Man, Little Man*, *Just Above My Head*, *The Evidence of Things Not Seen*, *Jimmy's Blues*, and *The Price of the Ticket*. Among the awards he received are a Eugene F. Saxon Memorial Trust Award, a Rosenwald Fellowship, a Guggenheim Fellowship, a *Partisan Review* Fellowship, and a Ford Foundation grant. He was made a Commander of the Legion of Honor in 1986. He died in 1987.

INTERNATIONAL

T0025847

ALSO BY JAMES BALDWIN

Nobody Knows
My Name

MORE NOTES OF A NATIVE SON

JAMES BALDWIN

VINTAGE INTERNATIONAL
Vintage Books
A Division of Random House, Inc.
New York

FIRST VINTAGE INTERNATIONAL EDITION, FEBRUARY 1993

Librrary of Congress Cataloging-in-Publication Data
Baldwin, James, 1924—
    Nobody knows my name / James Baldwin.
        p.   cm.
    Originally published: New York: Dial Press, 1961.
    ISBN 978-0-679-74473-3 (pbk.)
    1. Afro-Americans. 2. United States—Race relations. I. Title.
E185.61.B197   1993
305.896'073—dc20   92-50565
                                    CIP

Manufactured in the United States of America

for my brothers,
George, Wilmer
and
David

Acknowledgments

Acknowledgment is made to the following publications in whose pages these essays first appeared. *The New York Times Book Review* for "The Discovery of What It Means to Be an American" (January 25, 1959); *Encounter* for "Princes and Powers"; *Esquire* for "Fifth Avenue Uptown: a Letter from Harlem" (July, 1960), reprinted by permission; *New York Times Magazine* for "East River Downtown: Postscript to a Letter from Harlem" (which appeared as "A Negro Assays the Negro Mood," March 12, 1961); *Harper's Magazine* for "A Fly in Buttermilk" (which appeared as "The Hard Kind of Courage," October, 1958); *Partisan Review* for "Nobody Knows My Name: a Letter from the South" (Winter, 1959) and "Faulkner and Desegregation" (Winter, 1956); Kalamazoo College for "In Search of A Majority" delivered there as an address; *Esquire* for "Notes For A Hypothetical Novel" (delivered as an address at the third annual Esquire Magazine symposium on the "Role of the Writer in America" at San Francisco State College, October 22, 1960); *The New Leader* for "The Male Prison" (which appeared as "Gide As Husband and Homosexual," December 13, 1954); *Esquire* for "The Northern Protestant" (which appeared as "The Precarious Vogue of Ingmar Bergman," April, 1960), reprinted by permission; *The Reporter* for "Eight Men" (which appeared as "The Survival of Richard Wright," March 16, 1961); *Le Preuve* for "The Exile" (February, 1961); and *Esquire* for "The Black Boy Looks at The White Boy" (May, 1961), reprinted by permission.

Contents

Introduction

These essays were written over the last six years, in various places and in many states of mind. These years seemed, on the whole, rather sad and aimless to me. My life in Europe was ending, not because I had decided that it should, but because it became clearer and clearer —as I dealt with the streets, the climate, and the temperament of Paris, fled to Spain and Corsica and Scandinavia —that something had ended for me. I rather think now, to tell the sober truth, that it was merely my youth, first youth, anyway, that was ending and I hated to see it go. In the context of my life, the end of my youth was signaled by the reluctant realization that I had, indeed, become a writer; so far, so good: now I would have to go the distance.

In America, the color of my skin had stood between myself and me; in Europe, that barrier was down.

Nothing is more desirable than to be released from an affliction, but nothing is more frightening than to be divested of a crutch. It turned out that the question of who I was was not solved because I had removed myself from the social forces which menaced me—anyway, these forces had become interior, and I had dragged them across the ocean with me. The question of who I was had at last become a personal question, and the answer was to be found in me.

I think that there is always something frightening about this realization. I know it frightened me—that was one of the reasons that I dawdled in the European haven for so long. And yet, I could not escape the knowledge, though God knows I tried, that if I was still in need of havens, my journey had been for nothing. Havens are high-priced. The price exacted of the haven-dweller is that he contrive to delude himself into believing that he has found a haven. It would seem, unless one looks more deeply at the phenomenon, that most people are able to delude themselves and get through their lives quite happily. But I still believe that the unexamined life is not worth living: and I know that self-delusion, in the service of no matter what small or lofty cause, is a price no writer can afford. His subject is himself and the world and it requires every ounce of stamina he can summon to attempt to look on himself and the world as they are.

What it came to for me was that I no longer needed to fear leaving Europe, no longer needed to hide myself from the high and dangerous winds of the world. The world was enormous and I could go anywhere in it I chose—including America: and I decided to return here because I was afraid to. But the question which confronted me, nibbled at me, in my stony Corsican exile was: Am I afraid of returning to America? Or am I afraid of journeying any further with myself? Once this question had presented itself it would not be appeased, it had to be answered.

"Be careful what you set your heart upon," someone once said to me, "for it will surely be yours." Well, I had said that I was going to be a writer, God, Satan, and Mississippi notwithstanding, and that color did not matter, and that I was going to be free. And, here I was, left with only myself to deal with. It was entirely up to me.

These essays are a very small part of a private logbook. The question of color takes up much space in these pages, but the question of color, especially in this country, operates to hide the graver questions of the self. That is precisely why what we like to call "the Negro problem" is so tenacious in American life, and so dangerous. But my own experience proves to me that the connection between American whites and blacks is far deeper and more passionate than any of us like to think. And, even in icy Sweden, I found myself talking with a man whose endless questioning has given him himself, and who reminded me of black Baptist preachers. The

questions which one asks oneself begin, at last, to illumi-
nate the world, and become one's key to the experience
of others. One can only face in others what one can face
in oneself. On this confrontation depends the measure
of our wisdom and compassion. This energy is all that
one finds in the rubble of vanished civilizations, and the
only hope for ours.

                                          JAMES BALDWIN

PART ONE

Sitting in the House . . .

1. The Discovery of What It Means to Be an American

"IT IS A COMPLEX FATE TO BE AN American," Henry James observed, and the principal discovery an American writer makes in Europe is just how complex this fate is. America's history, her aspirations, her peculiar triumphs, her even more peculiar defeats, and her position in the world—yesterday and today—are all so profoundly and stubbornly unique that the very word "America" remains a new, almost completely undefined and extremely controversial proper noun. No one in the world seems to know exactly what it describes, not even we motley millions who call ourselves Americans.

I left America because I doubted my ability to survive the fury of the color problem here. (Sometimes I still do.) I wanted to prevent myself from becoming *merely* a Negro; or, even, merely a Negro writer. I wanted to find out in what way the *specialness* of my experience could be made to connect me with other people instead of dividing me from them. (I was as isolated from Negroes as I was from whites, which is what happens when a Negro begins, at bottom, to believe what white people say about him.)

In my necessity to find the terms on which my experience could be related to that of others, Negroes and whites, writers and non-writers, I proved, to my astonishment, to be as American as any Texas G.I. And I found my experience was shared by every American writer I knew in Paris. Like me, they had been divorced from their origins, and it turned out to make very little difference that the origins of white Americans were European and mine were African—they were no more at home in Europe than I was.

The fact that I was the son of a slave and they were the sons of free men meant less, by the time we confronted each other on European soil, than the fact that we were both searching for our separate identities. When we had found these, we seemed to be saying, why, then, we would no longer need to cling to the shame and bitterness which had divided us so long.

It became terribly clear in Europe, as it never had been here, that we knew more about each other than any European ever could. And it also became clear that, no matter where our fathers had been born, or what they had endured, the fact of Europe had formed us both was part of our identity and part of our inheritance.

I had been in Paris a couple of years before any of this became clear to me. When it did, I, like many a writer before me upon the discovery that his props have all been knocked out from under him, suffered a species of breakdown and was carried off to the mountains of Switzerland. There, in that absolutely alabaster landscape, armed with two Bessie Smith records and a typewriter, I began to try to re-create the life that I had first known as a child and from which I had spent so many years in flight.

It was Bessie Smith, through her tone and her cadence, who helped me to dig back to the way I myself must have spoken when I was a pickaninny, and to remember the things I had heard and seen and felt. I had buried them very deep. I had never listened to Bessie Smith in America (in the same way that, for years, I would not touch watermelon), but in Europe she helped to reconcile me to being a "nigger."

I do not think that I could have made this reconciliation here. Once I was able to accept my role—as distinguished, I must say, from my "place"—in the extraordinary drama which is America, I was released from the illusion that I hated America.

The story of what can happen to an American Negro writer in Europe simply illustrates, in some relief, what can happen to any American writer there. It is not meant, of course, to imply that it happens to them all, for Europe can be very crippling, too; and, anyway, a writer, when he has made his first breakthrough, has simply won a crucial skirmish in a dangerous, unending and unpredictable battle. Still, the breakthrough is important, and the point is that an American writer, in order to achieve it, very often has to leave this country.

The American writer, in Europe, is released, first of all, from the necessity of apologizing for himself. It is not until he *is* released from the habit of flexing his muscles and proving that he is just a "regular guy" that he realizes how crippling this habit has been. It is not necessary for him, there, to pretend to be something he is not, for the artist does not encounter in Europe the same suspicion he encounters here. Whatever the Europeans may actually think of artists, they have killed enough of them off by now to know that they are as real—and as persistent—as rain, snow, taxes or businessmen.

Of course, the reason for Europe's comparative clarity concerning the different functions of men in society is that European society has always been divided into classes in a way that American society never has been. A European writer considers himself to be part of an old and honorable tradition—of intellectual activity, of letters—and his choice of a vocation does not cause him any uneasy wonder as to whether or not it will cost him all his friends. But this tradition does not exist in America.

On the contrary, we have a very deep-seated distrust of real intellectual effort (probably because we suspect that it will destroy, as I hope it does, that myth of America to which we cling so desperately). An American writer fights his way to one of the lowest rungs on the American social ladder by means of pure bull-headedness and an indescribable series of odd jobs. He probably *has* been a "regular fellow" for much of his adult life, and it is not easy for him to step out of that lukewarm bath.

We must, however, consider a rather serious paradox: though American society is more mobile than Europe's, it is easier to cut across social and occupational lines there than it is here. This has something to do, I think, with the problem of status in American life. Where everyone has status, it is also perfectly possible, after all, that no one has. It seems inevitable, in any case, that a man may become uneasy as to just what his status is.

But Europeans have lived with the idea of status for a long time. A man can be as proud of being a good waiter as of being a good actor, and, in neither case, feel threatened. And this means that the actor and the waiter can have a freer and more genuinely friendly relationship in Europe than they are likely to have here. The waiter does not feel, with obscure resentment, that

the actor has "made it," and the actor is not tormented
by the fear that he may find himself, tomorrow, once
again a waiter.

This lack of what may roughly be called social paranoia causes the American writer in Europe to feel—
almost certainly for the first time in his life—that he
can reach out to everyone, that he is accessible to everyone and open to everything. This is an extraordinary
feeling. He feels, so to speak, his own weight, his own
value.

It is as though he suddenly came out of a dark tunnel
and found himself beneath the open sky. And, in fact,
in Paris, I began to see the sky for what seemed to be
the first time. It was borne in on me—and it did not
make me feel melancholy—that this sky had been there
before I was born and would be there when I was dead.
And it was up to me, therefore, to make of my brief opportunity the most that could be made.

I was born in New York, but have lived only in
pockets of it. In Paris, I lived in all parts of the city—on
the Right Bank and the Left, among the bourgeoisie
and among *les misérables*, and knew all kinds of people, from pimps and prostitutes in Pigalle to Egyptian
bankers in Neuilly. This may sound extremely unprin-
cipled or even obscurely immoral: I found it healthy. I
love to talk to people, all kinds of people, and almost
everyone, as I hope we still know, loves a man who loves
to listen.

This perpetual dealing with people very different from myself caused a shattering in me of preconceptions I scarcely knew I held. The writer is meeting in Europe people who are not American, whose sense of reality is entirely different from his own. They may love or hate or admire or fear or envy this country—they see it, in any case, from another point of view, and this forces the writer to reconsider many things he had always taken for granted. This reassessment, which can be very painful, is also very valuable.

This freedom, like all freedom, has its dangers and its responsibilities. One day it begins to be borne in on the writer, and with great force, that he is living in Europe as an American. If he were living there as a European, he would be living on a different and far less attractive continent.

This crucial day may be the day on which an Algerian taxi-driver tells him how it feels to be an Algerian in Paris. It may be the day on which he passes a café terrace and catches a glimpse of the tense, intelligent and troubled face of Albert Camus. Or it may be the day on which someone asks him to explain Little Rock and he begins to feel that it would be simpler—and, corny as the words may sound, more honorable—to *go* to Little Rock than sit in Europe, on an American passport, trying to explain it.

This is a personal day, a terrible day, the day to

which his entire sojourn has been tending. It is the day
he realizes that there are no untroubled countries in
this fearfully troubled world; that if he has been preparing himself for anything in Europe, he has been preparing himself—for America. In short, the freedom that
the American writer finds in Europe brings him, full
circle, back to himself, with the responsibility for his
development where it always was: in his own hands.

Even the most incorrigible maverick has to be born
somewhere. He may leave the group that produced
him—he may be forced to—but nothing will efface his
origins, the marks of which he carries with him everywhere. I think it is important to know this and even find
it a matter for rejoicing, as the strongest people do, regardless of their station. On this acceptance, literally,
the life of a writer depends.

The charge has often been made against American
writers that they do not describe society, and have no
interest in it. They only describe individuals in opposition to it, or isolated from it. Of course, what the American writer is describing is his own situation. But what
is *Anna Karenina* describing if not the tragic fate of
the isolated individual, at odds with her time and
place?

The real difference is that Tolstoy was describing an
old and dense society in which everything seemed—to
the people in it, though not to Tolstoy—to be fixed forever. And the book is a masterpiece because Tolstoy was

able to fathom, and make us see, the hidden laws which really governed this society and made Anna's doom inevitable.

American writers do not have a fixed society to describe. The only society they know is one in which nothing is fixed and in which the individual must fight for his identity. This is a rich confusion, indeed, and it creates for the American writer unprecedented opportunities.

That the tensions of American life, as well as the possibilities, are tremendous is certainly not even a question. But these are dealt with in contemporary literature mainly compulsively; that is, the book is more likely to be a symptom of our tension than an examination of it. The time has come, God knows, for us to examine ourselves, but we can only do this if we are willing to free ourselves of the myth of America and try to find out what is really happening here.

Every society is really governed by hidden laws, by unspoken but profound assumptions on the part of the people, and ours is no exception. It is up to the American writer to find out what these laws and assumptions are. In a society much given to smashing taboos without thereby managing to be liberated from them, it will be no easy matter.

It is no wonder, in the meantime, that the American writer keeps running off to Europe. He needs sustenance for his journey and the best models he can find. Europe

has what we do not have yet, a sense of the mysterious
and inexorable limits of life, a sense, in a word, of tragedy. And we have what they sorely need: a new sense
of life's possibilities.

In this endeavor to wed the vision of the Old World
with that of the New, it is the writer, not the statesman,
who is our strongest arm. Though we do not wholly believe it yet, the interior life is a real life, and the intan-
gible dreams of people have a tangible effect on the
world.

2. Princes and Powers

THE CONFERENCE OF NEGRO-AF-
rican Writers and Artists (*Le Congrès des Ecrivains et
Artistes Noirs*) opened on Wednesday, September 19,
1956, in the Sorbonne's Amphitheatre Descartes, in
Paris. It was one of those bright, warm days which one
likes to think of as typical of the atmosphere of the intellectual capital of the Western world. There were
people on the café terraces, boys and girls on the boule-
vards, bicycles racing by on their fantastically urgent
errands. Everyone and everything wore a cheerful aspect, even the houses of Paris, which did not show their
age. Those who were unable to pay the steep rents of
these houses were enabled, by the weather, to enjoy the
streets, to sit, unnoticed, in the parks. The boys and girls
and old men and women who had nowhere at all to go
and nothing whatever to do, for whom no provision had
been made, or could be, added to the beauty of the Paris

scene by walking along the river. The newspaper ven-
dors seemed cheerful; so did the people who bought the
newspapers. Even the men and women queueing up before bakeries—for there was a bread strike in Paris—
did so as though they had long been used to it.

The conference was to open at nine o'clock. By ten
o'clock the lecture hall was already unbearably hot,
people choked the entrances and covered the wooden
steps. It was hectic with the activity attendant upon the
setting up of tape recorders, with the testing of ear-
phones, with the lighting of flash-bulbs. Electricity, in
fact, filled the hall. Of the people there that first day, I
should judge that not quite two-thirds were colored.

Behind the table at the front of the hall sat eight
colored men. These included the American novelist
Richard Wright; Alioune Diop, the editor of *Présence
Africaine* and one of the principal organizers of the
conference; poets Leopold Senghor, from Senegal, and
Aimé Cesaire, from Martinique, and the poet and novelist Jacques Alexis, from Haiti. From Haiti, also, came
the President of the conference, Dr. Price-Mars, a very
old and very handsome man.

It was well past ten o'clock when the conference
actually opened. Alioune Diop, who is tall, very dark
and self-contained, and who rather resembles, in his
extreme sobriety, an old-time Baptist minister, made
the opening address. He referred to the present gather-
ing as a kind of second Bandung. As at Bandung, the

people gathered together here held in common the fact
of their subjugation to Europe, or, at the very least, to
the European vision of the world. Out of the fact that
European well-being had been, for centuries, so cru-
cially dependent on this subjugation had come that *ra-
cisme* from which all black men suffered. Then he spoke
of the changes which had taken place during the last
decade regarding the fate and the aspirations of non-
European peoples, especially the blacks. "The blacks,"
he said, "whom history has treated in a rather cavalier
fashion. I would even say that history has treated black
men in a resolutely spiteful fashion were it not for the
fact that this history with a large *H* is nothing more,
after all, than the Western interpretation of the life of
the world." He spoke of the variety of cultures the conference represented, saying that they were genuine cultures and that the ignorance of the West regarding them
was largely a matter of convenience.

Yet, in speaking of the relation between politics and
culture, he pointed out that the loss of vitality from
which all Negro cultures were suffering was due to the
fact that their political destinies were not in their hands.
A people deprived of political sovereignty finds it very
nearly impossible to recreate, for itself, the image of its
past, this perpetual recreation being an absolute necessity for, if not, indeed, the definition of a living culture.
And one of the questions, then, said Diop, which would
often be raised during this conference was the question

of assimilation. Assimilation was frequently but another name for the very special brand of relations between human beings which had been imposed by colonialism. These relations demanded that the individual, torn from the context to which he owed his identity, should replace his habits of feeling, thinking, and acting by another set of habits which belonged to the strangers who dominated him. He cited the example of certain natives of the Belgian Congo, who, *accablé des complexes*, wished for an assimilation so complete that they would no longer be distinguishable from white men. This, said Diop, indicated the blind horror which the spiritual heritage of Africa inspired in their breasts.

The question of assimilation could not, however, be posed this way. It was not a question, on the one hand, of simply being swallowed up, of disappearing in the maw of Western culture, nor was it, on the other hand, a question of rejecting assimilation in order to be isolated within African culture. Neither was it a question of deciding which African values were to be retained and which European values were to be adopted. Life was not that simple.

It was due to the crisis which their cultures were now undergoing that black intellectuals had come together. They were here to define and accept their responsibilities, to assess the riches and the promise of their cultures, and to open, in effect, a dialogue with Europe. He ended with a brief and rather moving reference to the fifteen-year struggle of himself and his confreres to bring about this day.

His speech won a great deal of applause. Yet, I felt that among the dark people in the hall there was, perhaps, some disappointment that he had not been more specific, more bitter, in a word, more demagogical; whereas, among the whites in the hall, there was certainly expressed in their applause a somewhat shame-faced and uneasy relief. And, indeed, the atmosphere was strange. No one, black or white, seemed quite to believe what was happening and everyone was tense with the question of which direction the conference would take. Hanging in the air, as real as the heat from which we suffered, were the great specters of America and Russia, of the battle going on between them for the domination of the world. The resolution of this battle might very well depend on the earth's non-European population, a population vastly outnumbering Europe's, and which had suffered such injustices at European hands. With the best will in the world, no one now living could undo what past generations had accomplished. The great question was what, exactly, *had* they accomplished: whether the evil, of which there had been so much, alone lived after them, whether the good, and there had been some, had been interred with their bones.

Of the messages from well-wishers which were read immediately after Diop's speech, the one which caused the greatest stir came from America's W. E. B. Du Bois.

"I am not present at your meeting," he began, "because the U.S. government will not give me a passport." The reading was interrupted at this point by great waves of laughter, by no means good-natured, and by a roar of applause, which, as it clearly could not have been intended for the State Department, was intended to express admiration for Du Bois' plain speaking. "Any American Negro traveling abroad today must either not care about Negroes or say what the State Department wishes him to say." This, of course, drew more applause. It also very neatly compromised whatever effectiveness the five-man American delegation then sitting in the hall might have hoped to have. It was less Du Bois' extremely ill-considered communication which did this than the incontestable fact that he had not been allowed to leave his country. It was a fact which could scarcely be explained or defended, particularly as one would have also had to explain just how the reasons for Du Bois' absence differed from those which had prevented the arrival of the delegation from South Africa. The very attempt at such an explanation, especially for people whose distrust of the West, however richly justified, also tends to make them dangerously blind and hasty, was to be suspected of "caring nothing about Negroes," of saying what the State Department "wished" you to say. It was a fact which increased and seemed to justify the distrust with which all Americans are regarded abroad, and it made yet deeper, for the five American Negroes present, that gulf which yawns between the American Negro and all other men of color. This is a very sad and dangerous state of affairs, for the American Negro is possibly the only man of color who can speak of the West with real authority, whose experience, painful as it is, also proves the vitality of the so transgressed Western ideals. The fact that Du Bois was not there and could not, therefore, be engaged in debate, naturally made the more seductive his closing argument: which was that, the future of Africa being socialist, African writers should take the road taken by Russia, Poland, China, etc., and not be "betrayed backward by the U.S. into colonialism."

When the morning session ended and I was spewed forth with the mob into the bright courtyard, Richard Wright introduced me to the American delegation. And it seemed quite unbelievable for a moment that the five men standing with Wright (and Wright and myself) were defined, and had been brought together in this courtyard by our relation to the African continent. The chief of the delegation, John Davis, was to be asked just *why* he considered himself a Negro—he was to be told that he certainly did not look like one. He *is* a Negro, of course, from the remarkable legal point of view which obtains in the United States, but, more importantly, as he tried to make clear to his interlocutor, he was a Negro by choice and by depth of involvement—by experience, in fact. But the question of choice in such a context can scarcely be coherent for an African and the experience referred to, which produces a John Davis, remains a closed book for him. Mr. Davis might have been rather darker, as were the others—Mercer Cook, William Fontaine, Horace Bond, and James Ivy —and it would not have helped matters very much.

For what, at bottom, distinguished the Americans from the Negroes who surrounded us, men from Nigeria, Senegal, Barbados, Martinique—so many names for so many disciplines—was the banal and abruptly quite overwhelming fact that we had been born in a society, which, in a way quite inconceivable for Africans, and no longer real for Europeans, was open, and, in a sense which has nothing to do with justice or injustice, was free. It was a society, in short, in which nothing was fixed and we had therefore been born to a greater number of possibilities, wretched as these possibilities seemed at the instant of our birth. Moreover, the land of our forefathers' exile had been made, by that travail, our home. It may have been the popular impulse to keep us at the bottom of the perpetually shifting and bewildered populace; but we were, on the other hand, almost personally indispensable to each of them, simply because, without us, they could never have been certain, in such a confusion, where the bottom was; and nothing, in any case, could take away our title to the land which we, too, had purchased with our blood. This results in a psychology very different—at its best and at its worst —from the psychology which is produced by a sense of

having been invaded and overrun, the sense of having
no recourse whatever against oppression other than over-
throwing the machinery of the oppressor. We had been
dealing with, had been made and mangled by, another
machinery altogether. It had never been in our interest
to overthrow it. It had been necessary to make the machinery work for our benefit and the possibility of its
doing so had been, so to speak, built in.

We could, therefore, in a way, be considered the connecting link between Africa and the West, the most real
and certainly the most shocking of all African contributions to Western cultural life. The articulation of this
reality, however, was another matter. But it was clear
that our relation to the mysterious continent of Africa
would not be clarified until we had found some means
of saying, to ourselves and to the world, more about the
mysterious American continent than had ever been said
before.

M. Lasebikan, from Nigeria, spoke that afternoon on
the tonal strucure of Youriba poetry, a language
spoken by five million people in his country. Lasebikan
was a very winning and unassuming personality, dressed
in a most arresting costume. What looked like a white
lace poncho covered him from head to foot; beneath
this he was wearing a very subdued but very ornately
figured silk robe, which looked Chinese, and he wore a

red velvet toque, a sign, someone told me, that he was a Mohammedan.

The Youriba language, he told us, had only become a written language in the middle of the last century and this had been done by missionaries. His face expressed some sorrow at this point, due, it developed, to the fact that this had not already been accomplished by the Youriba people. However—and his face brightened again—he lived in the hope that one day an excavation would bring to light a great literature written by the Youriba people. In the meantime, with great good nature, he resigned himself to sharing with us that literature which already existed. I doubt that I learned much about the tonal structure of Youriba poetry, but I found myself fascinated by the sensibility which had produced it. M. Lasebikan spoke first in Youriba and then in English. It was perhaps because he so clearly loved his subject that he not only succeeded in conveying the poetry of this extremely strange language, he also conveyed something of the style of life out of which it came. The poems quoted ranged from the devotional to a poem which described the pounding of yams. And one somehow felt the loneliness and the yearning of the first and the peaceful, rhythmic domesticity of the second. There was a poem about the memory of a battle, a poem about a faithless friend, and a poem celebrating the variety to be found in life, which conceived of this variety in rather startling terms: "Some would have been great eaters, but

they haven't got the food; some, great drinkers, but they
haven't got the wine." Some of the poetry demanded
the use of a marvelously ornate drum, on which were
many little bells. It was not the drum it once had been,
he told us, but despite whatever mishap had befallen it, I
could have listened to him play it for the rest of the
afternoon.

He was followed by Leopold Senghor. Senghor is a
very dark and impressive figure in a smooth, bespec-
tacled kind of way, and he is very highly regarded as a
poet. He was to speak on West African writers and
artists.

He began by invoking what he called the "spirit of
Bandung." In referring to Bandung, he was referring
less, he said, to the liberation of black peoples than he
was saluting the reality and the toughness of their culture, which, despite the vicissitudes of their history, had
refused to perish. We were now witnessing, in fact,
the beginning of its renaissance. This renaissance would
owe less to politics than it would to black writers and
artists. The "spirit of Bandung" had had the effect of
"sending them to school to Africa."

One of the things, said Senghor—perhaps *the* thing—
which distinguishes Africans from Europeans is the
comparative urgency of their ability to feel. *"Sentir c'est
apercevoir"*: it is perhaps a tribute to his personal force
that this phrase then meant something which makes the
literal English translation quite inadequate, seeming to

leave too great a distance between the feeling and the perception. The feeling and the perception, for Africans, is one and the same thing. This is the difference between European and African reasoning: the reasoning of the African is not compartmentalized, and, to illustrate this, Senghor here used the image of the bloodstream in which all things mingle and flow to and through the heart. He told us that the difference between the function of the arts in Europe and their function in Africa lay in the fact that, in Africa, the function of the arts is more present and pervasive, is infinitely less special, "is done by all, for all." Thus, art for art's sake is not a concept which makes any sense in Africa. The division between art and life out of which such a concept comes does not exist there. Art itself is taken to be perishable, to be made again each time it disappears or is destroyed. What is clung to is the spirit which makes art possible. And the African idea of this spirit is very different from the European idea. European art attempts to imitate nature. African art is concerned with reaching beyond and beneath nature, to contact, and itself become a part of *la force vitale*. The artistic image is not intended to represent the thing itself, but, rather, the reality of the force the thing contains. Thus, the moon is fecundity, the elephant is force.

Much of this made great sense to me, even though Senghor was speaking of, and out of, a way of life which I could only very dimly and perhaps somewhat wistfully imagine. It was the esthetic which attracted me, the idea that the work of art expresses, contains, and is itself a part of that energy which is life. Yet, I was aware that Senghor's thought had come into my mind translated. What he had been speaking of was something more direct and less isolated than the line in which my imagination immediately began to move. The distortions used by African artists to create a work of art are not at all the same distortions which have become one of the principal aims of almost every artist in the West today. (They are not the same distortions even when they have been copied from Africa.) And this was due entirely to the different situations in which each had his being. Poems and stories, in the only situation I know anything about, were never told, except, rarely, to children, and, at the risk of mayhem, in bars. They were written to be read, alone, and by a handful of people at that—there was really beginning to be something suspect in being read by more than a handful. These creations no more insisted on the actual presence of other human beings than they demanded the collaboration of a dancer and a drum. They could not be said to celebrate the society any more than the homage which Western artists sometimes receive can be said to have anything to do with society's celebration of a work of art. The only thing in Western life which seemed even faintly to approximate Senghor's intense sketch of the creative interdependence, the active, actual, joyful inter-

course obtaining among African artists and what only a
Westerner would call their public, was the atmosphere
sometimes created among jazz musicians and their fans
during, say, a jam session. But the ghastly isolation of
the jazz musician, the neurotic intensity of his listeners,
was proof enough that what Senghor meant when he
spoke of social art had no reality whatever in Western
life. He was speaking out of his past, which had been
lived where art was naturally and spontaneously social,
where artistic creation did not presuppose divorce. (Yet
he was not there. Here he was, in Paris, speaking the
adopted language in which he also wrote his poetry.)

Just what the specific relation of an artist to his culture says about that culture is a very pretty question.
The culture which had produced Senghor seemed, on the
face of it, to have a greater coherence as regarded
assumptions, traditions, customs, and beliefs than did
the Western culture to which it stood in so problematical
a relation. And this might very well mean that the culture represented by Senghor was healthier than the culture represented by the hall in which he spoke. But the
leap to this conclusion, than which nothing would have
seemed easier, was frustrated by the question of just
what health is in relation to a culture. Senghor's culture, for example, did not seem to need the lonely activity of the singular intelligence on which the cultural life
—the moral life—of the West depends. And a really
cohesive society, one of the attributes, perhaps, of what

is taken to be a "healthy" culture, has, generally, and, I suspect, necessarily, a much lower level of tolerance for the maverick, the dissenter, the man who steals the fire, than have societies in which, the common ground of belief having all but vanished, each man, in awful and brutal isolation, is for himself, to flower or to perish. Or, not impossibly, to make real and fruitful again that vanished common ground, which, as I take it, is nothing more or less than the culture itself, endangered and rendered nearly inaccessible by the complexities it has, itself, inevitably created.

Nothing is more undeniable than the fact that cultures vanish, undergo crises; are, in any case, in a perpetual state of change and fermentation, being perpetually driven, God knows where, by forces within and without. And one of the results, surely, of the present tension between the society represented by Senghor and the society represented by the Salle Descartes was just this perceptible drop, during the last decade, of the Western level of tolerance. I wondered what this would mean— for Africa, for us. I wondered just what effect the concept of art expressed by Senghor would have on that renaissance he had predicted and just what transformations this concept itself would undergo as it encountered the complexities of the century into which it was moving with such speed.

The evening debate rang perpetual changes on two questions. These questions—each of which splintered, each time it was asked, into a thousand more—were, first: What *is* a culture? This is a difficult question under the most serene circumstances—under which circumstances, incidentally, it mostly fails to present itself. (This implies, perhaps, one of the possible definitions of a culture, at least at a certain stage of its development.) In the context of the conference, it was a question which was helplessly at the mercy of another one. And the second question was this: Is it possible to describe as a culture what may simply be, after all, a history of oppression? That is, is this history and these present facts, which involve so many millions of people who are divided from each other by so many miles of the globe, which operates, and has operated, under such very different conditions, to such different effects, and which has produced so many different subhistories, problems, traditions, possibilities, aspirations, assumptions, languages, hybrids—is this history enough to have made of the earth's black populations anything that can legitimately be described as a culture? For what, beyond the fact that all black men at one time or another left Africa, or have remained there, do they really have in common?

And yet, it became clear as the debate wore on, that there *was* something which all black men held in common, something which cut across opposing points of

view, and placed in the same context their widely dis-
similiar experience. What they held in common was
their precarious, their unutterably painful relation to
the white world. What they held in common was the
necessity to remake the world in their own image, to
impose this image on the world, and no longer be
controlled by the vision of the world, and of themselves,
held by other people. What, in sum, black men held in
common was their ache to come into the world as men.
And this ache united people who might otherwise have
been divided as to what a man should be.

Yet, whether or not this could properly be described
as a *cultural* reality remained another question. Haiti's
Jacques Alexis made the rather desperate observation
that a cultural survey must have *something* to survey;
but then seemed confounded, as, indeed, we all were,
by the dimensions of the particular cultural survey in
progress. It was necessary, for example, before one
could relate the culture of Haiti to that of Africa, to
know what the Haitian culture was. Within Haiti there
were a great many cultures. Frenchmen, Negroes, and
Indians had bequeathed it quite dissimilar ways of life;
Catholics, voodooists, and animists cut across class and
color lines. Alexis described as "pockets" of culture
those related and yet quite specific and dissimilar ways
of life to be found within the borders of any country
in the world and wished to know by what alchemy
these opposing ways of life became a national culture.

And he wished to know, too, what relation national culture bore to national independence—was it possible,
really, to speak of a national culture when speaking
of nations which were not free?

Senghor remarked, apropos of this question, that one
of the great difficulties posed by this problem of cultures within cultures, particularly within the borders of
Africa herself, was the difficulty of establishing and
maintaining contact with the people if one's language
had been formed in Europe. And he went on, somewhat
later, to make the point that the heritage of the American Negro was an African heritage. He used, as proof
of this, a poem of Richard Wright's which was, he
said, involved with African tensions and symbols, even
though Wright himself had not been aware of this. He
suggested that the study of African sources might
prove extremely illuminating for American Negroes.
For, he suggested, in the same way that white classics
exist—classic here taken to mean an enduring revelation and statement of a specific, peculiar, cultural sensibility—black classics must also exist. This raised in
my mind the question of whether or not white classics
did exist, and, with this question, I began to see the
implications of Senghor's claim.

For, if white classics existed, in distinction, that is,
to merely French or English classics, these could only
be the classics produced by Greece and Rome. If *Black
Boy*, said Senghor, were to be analyzed, it would un-

doubtedly reveal the African heritage to which it owed
its existence; in the same way, I supposed, that Dickens'
A Tale Of Two Cities, would, upon analysis, reveal its
debt to Aeschylus. It did not seem very important.

And yet, I realized, the question had simply never
come up in relation to European literature. It was not,
now, the European necessity to go rummaging in the
past, and through all the countries of the world, bitterly
staking out claims to its cultural possessions.

Yet *Black Boy* owed its existence to a great many
other factors, by no means so tenuous or so problematical; in so handsomely presenting Wright with his African heritage, Senghor rather seemed to be taking away
his identity. *Black Boy* is the study of the growing up
of a Negro boy in the Deep South, and is one of the
major American autobiographies. I had never thought
of it, as Senghor clearly did, as one of the major
African autobiographies, only one more document, in
fact, like one more book in the Bible, speaking of the
African's long persecution and exile.

Senghor chose to overlook several gaps in his argument, not the least of which was the fact that Wright
had not been in a position, as Europeans had been, to
remain in contact with his hypothetical African heritage.
The Greco-Roman tradition had, after all, been *written
down;* it was by this means that it had kept itself alive.
Granted that there was something African in *Black Boy,*
as there was undoubtedly something African in all

American Negroes, the great question of what this was, and how it had survived, remained wide open. Moreover, *Black Boy* had been written in the English language which Americans had inherited from England, that is, if you like, from Greece and Rome; its form, psychology, moral attitude, preoccupations, in short, its cultural validity, were all due to forces which had nothing to do with Africa. Or was it simply that we had been rendered unable to recognize Africa in it?—for, it seemed that, in Senghor's vast re-creation of the world, the footfall of the African would prove to have covered more territory than the footfall of the Roman.

Thursday's great event was Aimé Cesaire's speech in the afternoon, dealing with the relation between colonization and culture. Cesaire is a caramel-colored man from Martinique, probably around forty, with a great tendency to roundness and smoothness, physically speaking, and with the rather vaguely benign air of a schoolteacher. All this changes the moment he begins to speak. It becomes at once apparent that his curious, slow-moving blandness is related to the grace and patience of a jungle cat and that the intelligence behind those spectacles is of a very penetrating and demagogic order.

The cultural crisis through which we are passing today can be summed up thus, said Cesaire: that culture which is strongest from the material and technological point of view threatens to crush all weaker cultures, particularly in a world in which, distance counting for nothing, the technologically weaker cultures have no means of protecting themselves. All cultures have, furthermore, an economic, social, and political base, and no culture can continue to live if its political destiny is not in its own hands. "Any political and social regime which destroys the self-determination of a people also destroys the creative power of that people." When this has happened the culture of that people has been destroyed. And it is simply not true that the colonizers bring to the colonized a new culture to replace the old one, a culture not being something given to a people, but, on the contrary and by definition, something that they make themselves. Nor is it, in any case, in the nature of colonialism to wish or to permit such a degree of well-being among the colonized. The well-being of the colonized is desirable only insofar as this well-being enriches the dominant country, the necessity of which is simply to remain dominant. Now the civilizations of Europe, said Cesaire, speaking very clearly and intensely to a packed and attentive hall, evolved an economy based on capital and the capital was based on black labor; and thus, regardless of whatever arguments Europeans use to defend themselves, and in spite of the absurd palliatives with which they have sometimes tried to soften the blow, the fact, of their domination, in order to accomplish and maintain this domination—in order, in fact, to make money—they destroyed, with utter ruthlessness, everything that stood in their way, languages, customs, tribes, lives; and not only put nothing in its place, but erected, on the contrary, the most tremendous barriers between themselves and the people they ruled. Europeans never had the remotest intention of raising Africans to the Western level, of sharing with them the instruments of physical, political or economic power. It was precisely their intention, their necessity, to keep the people they ruled in a state of cultural anarchy, that is, simply in a barbaric state. "The famous inferiority complex one is pleased to observe as a characteristic of the colonized is no accident but something very definitely desired and deliberately inculcated by the colonizer." He was interrupted at this point—not for the first time—by long and prolonged applause.

"The situation, therefore, in the colonial countries, is tragic," Cesaire continued. "Wherever colonization is a fact the indigenous culture begins to rot. And, among these ruins, something begins to be born which is not a culture but a kind of subculture, a subculture which is condemned to exist on the margin allowed it by European culture. This then becomes the province of a few men, the elite, who find themselves placed in the most artificial conditions, deprived of any revivifying contact with the masses of the people. Under such conditions, this subculture has no chance whatever of growing into an active, living culture." And what, he asked, before this situation, can be done?

The answer would not be simple. "In every society there is always a delicate balance between the old and the new, a balance which is perpetually being re-established, which is re-established by each generation. Black societies, cultures, civilizations, will not escape this law." Cesaire spoke of the energy already proved by black cultures in the past, and, declining to believe that this energy no longer existed, declined also to believe that the total obliteration of the existing culture was a condition for the renaissance of black people. "In the culture to be born there will no doubt be old and new elements. How these elements will be mixed is not a question to which any individual can respond. The response must be given by the community. But we can say this: that the response will be given, and not verbally, but in tangible facts, and by action."

He was interrupted by applause again. He paused, faintly smiling, and reached his peroration: "We find ourselves today in a cultural chaos. And this is our role: to liberate the forces which, alone, can organize from this chaos a new synthesis, a synthesis which will deserve the name of a culture, a synthesis which will be the reconciliation—*et dépassement*—of the old and the new. We are here to proclaim the right of our people to speak, to let our people, black people, make their entrance on the great stage of history."

This speech, which was very brilliantly delivered, and which had the further advantage of being, in the main, unanswerable (and the advantage, also, of being very little concerned, at bottom, with culture) wrung from the audience which heard it the most violent reaction of joy. Cesaire had spoken for those who could not speak and those who could not speak thronged around the table to shake his hand, and kiss him. I myself felt stirred in a very strange and disagreeable way. For Cesaire's case against Europe, which was watertight, was also a very easy case to make. The anatomizing of the great injustice which is the irreducible fact of colonialism was yet not enough to give the victims of that injustice a new sense of themselves. One may say, of course, that the very fact that Cesaire had spoken so thrillingly, and in one of the great institutions of Western learning, invested them with this new sense, but I do not think this is so. He had certainly played very skillfully on their emotions and their hopes, but he had not raised the central, tremendous question, which was, simply: What *had* this colonial experience made of them and what were they now to do with it? For they were all, now, whether they liked it or not, related to Europe, stained by European visions and standards, and their relation to themselves, and to each other, and to their past had changed. Their relation to their poets had also changed, as had the relation of their poets to them. Cesaire's speech left out of account one of the great effects of the colonial experience: its creation, precisely, of men like himself. His real relation to the people who thronged about him now had been changed, by this experience, into something very different from what it once had been. What made him so attractive now was the fact that he, without having ceased to be one of them, yet seemed to move with the European authority. He had penetrated into the heart of the great wilderness which was Europe and stolen the sacred fire. And this, which was the promise of their freedom, was also the assurance of his power.

Friday's session began in a rather tense atmosphere and this tension continued throughout the day. Diop opened the session by pointing out that each speaker spoke only for himself and could not be considered as speaking for the conference. I imagined that this had something to with Cesaire's speech of the day before and with some of its effects, among which, apparently, had been a rather sharp exchange between Cesaire and the American delegation.

This was the session during which it became apparent that there was a religious war going on at the conference, a war which suggested, in miniature, some of the tensions dividing Africa. A Protestant minister from the Cameroons, Pastor T. Ekollo, had been forced by the hostility of the audience the day before to abandon a dissertation in defense of Christianity in

Africa. He was visibly upset still. "There will be Christians in Africa, even when there is not a white man there," he said, with a tense defiance, and added, with an unconsciously despairing irony to which, however, no one reacted, "supposing that to be possible." He had been asked how he could defend Christianity in view of what Christians had done in his country. To which his answer was that the doctrine of Christianity was of more moment than the crimes committed by Christians. The necessity which confronted Africans was to make Christianity real in their own lives, without reference to the crimes committed by others. The audience was extremely cold and hostile, forcing him again, in effect, from the floor. But I felt that this also had something to do with Pastor Ekollo's rather petulant and not notably Christian attitude toward them.

Dr. Marcus James, a priest of the Anglican church from Jamaica, picked up where Ekollo left off. Dr. James is a round, very pleasant-looking, chocolate-colored man, with spectacles. He began with a quotation to the effect that, when the Christian arrived in Africa, he had the Bible and the African had the land; but that, before long, the African had the Bible and the Christian had the land. There was a great deal of laughter at this, in which Dr. James joined. But the postscript to be added today, he said, is that the African not only has the Bible but has found in it a potential weapon for the recovery of his land. The Christians in the hall, who seemed to be in the minority, applauded and stomped their feet at this, but many others now rose and left.

Dr. James did not seem to be distressed and went on to discuss the relationship between Christianity and democracy. In Africa, he said, there was none whatever. Africans do not, in fact, believe that Christianity is any longer real for Europeans, due to the immense scaffolding with which they have covered it, and the fact that this religion has no effect whatever on their conduct. There are, nevertheless, more than twenty million Christians in Africa, and Dr. James believed that the future of their country was very largely up to them. The task of making Christianity real in Africa was made the more difficult in that they could expect no help whatever from Europe: "Christianity, as practiced by Europeans in Africa, is a cruel travesty."

This bitter observation, which was uttered in sorrow, gained a great deal of force from the fact that so genial a man had felt compelled to make it. It made vivid, unanswerable, in a way which rage could not have done, how little the West has respected its own ideals in dealing with subject peoples, and suggested that there was a price we would pay for this. He speculated a little on what African Christianity might become, and how it might contribute to the rebirth of Christianity everywhere; and left his audience to chew on this momentous speculation: Considering, he

said, that what Africa wishes to wrest from Europe is
power, will it be necessary for Africa to take the same
bloody road which Europe has followed? Or will it be
possible for her to work out some means of avoiding
this?

M. Wahal, from the Sudan, spoke in the afternoon
on the role of the law in culture, using as an illustration the role the law had played in the history of the
American Negro. He spoke at length on the role of
French law in Africa, pointing out that French law is
simply not equipped to deal with the complexity of the
African situation. And what is even worse, of course,
is that it makes virtually no attempt to do so. The result is that French law, in Africa, is simply a legal
means of administering injustice. It is not a solution,
either, simply to revert to African tribal custom, which
is also helpless before the complexities of present-day
African life. Wahal spoke with a quiet matter-of-fact-
ness, which lent great force to the ugly story he was
telling, and he concluded by saying that the question
was ultimately a political one and that there was no
hope of solving it within the framework of the present
colonial system.

He was followed by George Lamming. Lamming is
tall, raw-boned, untidy, and intense, and one of his
real distinctions is his refusal to be intimidated by the
fact that he is a genuine writer. He proposed to raise
certain questions pertaining to the quality of life to be

lived by black people in that hypothetical tomorrow when they would no longer be ruled by whites. "The profession of letters is an untidy one," he began, looking as though he had dressed to prove it. He directed his speech to Aimé Cesaire and Jacques Alexis in particular, and quoted Djuna Barnes: "Too great a sense of identity makes a man feel he can do no wrong. And too little does the same." He suggested that it was important to bear in mind that the word Negro meant black—and meant nothing more than that; and commented on the great variety of heritages, experiences, and points of view which the conference had brought together under the heading of this single noun. He wished to suggest that the nature of power was unrelated to pigmentation, that bad faith was a phenomenon which was independent of race. He found—from the point of view of an untidy man of letters—something crippling in the obsession from which Negroes suffered as regards the existence and the attitudes of the Other—this Other being everyone who was not Negro. That black people faced great problems was surely not to be denied and yet the greatest problem facing us was what *we*, Negroes, would do among ourselves "when there was no longer any colonial horse to ride." He pointed out that this was the horse on which a great many Negroes, who were in what he called "the skin trade," hoped to ride to power, power which would

be in no way distinguishable from the power they sought
to overthrow.

Lamming was insisting on the respect which is due
the private life. I respected him very much, not only
because he raised this question, but because he knew
what he was doing. He was concerned with the immen-
sity and the variety of the experience called Negro; he
was concerned that one should recognize this variety
as wealth. He cited the case of Amos Tutuola's *The
Palm-Wine Drinkard*, which he described as a fantasy,
made up of legends, anecdotes, episodes, the product,
in fact, of an oral story-telling tradition which disap-
peared from Western life generations ago. Yet "Tutuola really *does* speak English. It is *not* his second language." The English did not find the book strange. On
the contrary, they were astonished by how truthfully it
seemed to speak to them of their own experience. They
felt that Tutuola was closer to the English than he could
possibly be to his equivalent in Nigeria; and yet Tutuola's work could elicit this reaction only because, in a
way which could never really be understood, but which
Tutuola had accepted, he was closer to his equivalent
in Nigeria than he would ever be to the English. It
seemed to me that Lamming was suggesting to the conference a subtle and difficult idea, the idea that part of
the great wealth of the Negro experience lay precisely
in its double-edgedness. He was suggesting that all Negroes were held in a state of supreme tension between

the difficult, dangerous relationship in which they stood to the white world and the relationship, not a whit less painful or dangerous, in which they stood to each other. He was suggesting that in the acceptance of this duality lay their strength, that in this, precisely, lay their means of defining and controlling the world in which they lived.

Lamming was interrupted at about this point, however, for it had lately been decided, in view of the great number of reports still to be read, to limit everyone to twenty minutes. This quite unrealistic rule was not to be observed very closely, especially as regarded the French-speaking delegates. But Lamming put his notes in his pocket and ended by saying that if, as someone had remarked, silence was the only common language, politics, for Negroes, was the only common ground.

The evening session began with a film, which I missed, and was followed by a speech from Cheik Anta Diop, which, in sum, claimed the ancient Egyptian empire as part of the Negro past. I can only say that this question has never greatly exercised my mind, nor did M. Diop succeed in doing so—at least not in the direction he intended. He quite refused to remain within the twenty-minute limit and, while his claims of the deliberate dishonesty of all Egyptian scholars may be quite well founded for all I know, I cannot say that he convinced me. He was, however, a great success in the hall, second only, in fact, to Aimé Cesaire.

He was followed by Richard Wright. Wright had been acting as liaison man between the American delegation and the Africans and this had placed him in rather a difficult position, since both factions tended to claim him as their spokesman. It had not, of course, occurred to the Americans that he could be anything less, whereas the Africans automatically claimed him because of his great prestige as a novelist and his reputation for calling a spade a spade—particularly if the spade were white. The consciousness of his peculiar and certainly rather grueling position weighed on him, I think, rather heavily.

He began by confessing that the paper he had written, while on his farm in Normandy, impressed him as being, after the events of the last few days, inadequate. Some of the things he had observed during the course of the conference had raised questions in him which his paper could not have foreseen. He had not, however, rewritten his paper, but would read it now, exactly as it had been written, interrupting himself whenever what he had written and what he had since been made to feel seemed to be at variance. He was exposing, in short, his conscience to the conference and asking help of them in his confusion.

There was, first of all, he said, a painful contradiction in being at once a Westerner and a black man. "I see both worlds from another, and third, point of view." This fact had nothing to do with his will, his desire, or his choice. It was simply that he had been born in the West and the West had formed him.

As a black Westerner, it was difficult to know what one's attitude should be toward three realities which were inextricably woven together in the Western fabric. These were religion, tradition, and imperialism, and in none of these realities had the lives of black men been taken into account: their advent dated back to 1455, when the church had determined to rule all infidels. And it just so happened, said Wright, ironically, that a vast proportion of these infidels were black. Nevertheless, this decision on the part of the church had not been, despite the church's intentions, entirely oppressive, for one of the results of 1455 had, at length, been Calvin and Luther, who shook the authority of the church in insisting on the authority of the individual conscience. This might not, he said accurately, have been precisely their intention, but it had certainly been one of their effects. For, with the authority of the church shaken, men were left prey to many strange and new ideas, ideas which led, finally, to the discrediting of the racial dogma. Neither had this been foreseen, but what men imagine they are doing and what they are doing in fact are rarely the same thing. This was a perfectly valid observation which would, I felt, have been just as valid without the remarkable capsule history with which Wright imagined he supported it.

Wright then went on to speak of the effects of Eu-

ropean colonialism in the African colonies. He con-
fessed—bearing in mind always the great gap between
human intentions and human effects—that he thought
of it as having been, in many ways, liberating, since it
smashed old traditions and destroyed old gods. One of
the things that surprised him in the last few days had
been the realization that most of the delegates to the
conference did not feel as he did. He felt, nevertheless,
that, though Europeans had not realized what they were
doing in freeing Africans from the "rot" of their past,
they had been accomplishing a good. And yet—he was
not certain that he had the right to say that, having
forgotten that Africans are not American Negroes and
were not, therefore, as he somewhat mysteriously considered American Negroes to be, free from their "irrational" past.

In sum, Wright said, he felt that Europe had brought
the Enlightenment to Africa and that "what was good
for Europe was good for all mankind." I felt that this
was, perhaps, a tactless way of phrasing a debatable
idea, but Wright went on to express a notion which I
found even stranger. And this was that the West, having created an African and Asian elite, should now
"give them their heads" and "refuse to be shocked" at
the "methods they will feel compelled to use" in unify-
ing their countries. We had not, ourselves, used very
pretty methods. Presumably, this left us in no position to
throw stones at Nehru, Nasser, Sukarno, etc., should

they decide, as they almost surely would, to use dic-
tatorial methods in order to hasten the "social evolu-
tion." In any case, Wright said, these men, the leaders
of their countries, once the new social order was established, would voluntarily surrender the "personal
power." He did not say what would happen then, but I
supposed it would be the second coming.

Saturday was the last day of the conference, which
was scheduled to end with the invitation to the audience
to engage with the delegates in the Euro-African dialogue. It was a day marked by much confusion and
excitement and discontent—this last on the part of people who felt that the conference had been badly run, or
who had not been allowed to read their reports. (They
were often the same people.) It was marked, too, by
rather a great deal of plain speaking, both on and off,
but mostly off, the record. The hall was even more hot
and crowded than it had been the first day and the
photographers were back.

The entire morning was taken up in an attempt to
agree on a "cultural inventory." This had to be done
before the conference could draft those resolutions which
they were, today, to present to the world. This task
would have been extremely difficult even had there obtained in the black world a greater unity—geographical,
spiritual, and historical—than is actually the case.
Under the circumstances, it was an endeavor compli-

cated by the nearly indefinable complexities of the word
culture, by the fact that no coherent statement had
yet been made concerning the relationship of black cultures to each other, and, finally, by the necessity, which
had obtained throughout the conference, of avoiding
the political issues.

The inability to discuss politics had certainly handicapped the conference, but it could scarcely have been
run otherwise. The political question would have caused
the conference to lose itself in a war of political ideol-
ogies. Moreover, the conference *was* being held in Paris,
many of the delegates represented areas which belonged
to France, most of them represented areas which were
not free. There was also to be considered the delicate
position of the American delegation, which had sat
throughout the conference uncomfortably aware that
they might at any moment be forced to rise and leave
the hall.

The declaration of political points of view being
thus prohibited, the "cultural" debate which raged in
the hall that morning was in perpetual danger of drowning in the sea of the unstated. For, according to his
political position, each delegate had a different interpretation of his culture, and a different idea of its future,
as well as the means to be used to make that future a
reality. A solution of a kind was offered by Senghor's
suggestion that two committees be formed, one to take
an inventory of the past, and one to deal with present

prospects. There was some feeling that two committees were scarcely necessary. Diop suggested that one committee be formed, which, if necessary, could divide itself into two. Then the question arose as to just how the committee should be appointed, whether by countries or by cultural areas. It was decided, at length, that the committee should be set up on the latter basis, and should have resolutions drafted by noon. "It is by these resolutions," protested Mercer Cook, "that we shall make ourselves known. It cannot be done in an hour."

He was entirely right. At eleven-twenty a committee of eighteen members had been formed. At four o'clock in the afternoon they were still invisible. By this time, too, the most tremendous impatience reigned in the crowded hall, in which, today, Negroes by far outnumbered whites. At four-twenty-five the impatience of the audience erupted in whistles, catcalls, and stamping of feet. At four-thirty, Alioune Diop arrived and officially opened the meeting. He tried to explain some of the difficulties such a conference inevitably encountered and assured the audience that the committee on resolutions would not be absent much longer. In the meantime, in their absence, and in the absence of Dr. Price-Mars, he proposed to read a few messages from well-wishers. But the audience was not really interested in these messages and was manifesting a very definite tendency to get out of hand again when, at four-fifty-five, Dr. Price-Mars entered. His arrival had the effect of

calming the audience somewhat and, luckily, the committee on resolutions came in very shortly afterwards.
At five-seven, Diop rose to read the document which had
come one vote short of being unanimously approved.

As is the way with documents of this kind, it was
carefully worded and slightly repetitious. This did not
make its meaning less clear or diminish its importance.

It spoke first of the great importance of the cultural
inventory here begun in relation to the various black
cultures which had been "systematically misunderstood,
underestimated, sometimes destroyed." This inventory
had confirmed the pressing need for a re-examination
of the history of these cultures (*"la verité historique"*)
with a view to their re-evaluation. The ignorance concerning them, the errors, and the willful distortions,
were among the great contributing factors to the crisis
through which they now were passing, in relation to
themselves and to human culture in general. The active
aid of writers, artists, theologians, thinkers, scientists,
and technicians was necessary for the revival, the reha-
bilitation, and the development of these cultures as the
first step toward their integration in the active cultural
life of the world. Black men, whatever their political
and religious beliefs, were united in believing that the
health and growth of these cultures could not possibly
come about until colonialism, the exploitation of un-
developed peoples, and racial discrimination had come
to an end. (At this point the conference expressed its

regret at the involuntary absence of the South African delegation and the reading was interrupted by prolonged and violent applause.) All people, the document continued, had the right to be able to place themselves in fruitful contact with their national cultural values and to benefit from the instruction and education which could be afforded them within this framework. It spoke of the progress which had taken place in the world in the last few years and stated that this progress permitted one to hope for the general abolition of the colonial system and the total and universal end of racial discrimination, and ended: "Our conference, which respects the cultures of all countries and appreciates their contributions to the progress of civilization, engages all black men in the defense, the illustration, and the dissemination throughout the world of the national values of their people. We, black writers and artists, proclaim our brotherhood toward all men and expect of them (*'nous attendons d'eux'*) the manifestation of this same brotherhood toward our people."

When the applause in which the last words of this document were very nearly drowned had ended, Diop pointed out that this was not a declaration of war; it was, rather, he said, a declaration of love—for the culture, European, which had been of such importance in the history of mankind. But it had been very keenly felt that it was now necessary for black men to make the effort to define themselves *au lieu d'être toujours defini par les autres.* Black men had resolved "to take their destinies into their own hands." He spoke of plans for the setting up of an international association for the dissemination of black culture and, at five-twenty-two, Dr. Price-Mars officially closed the conference and opened the floor to the audience for the Euro-African dialogue.

Someone, a European, addressed this question to Aimé Cesaire: How, he asked, do you explain the fact that many Europeans—as well as many Africans, *bien entendu*—reject what is referred to as European culture? A European himself, he was far from certain that such a thing as a European culture existed. It was possible to be a European without accepting the Greco-Roman tradition. Neither did he believe in race. He wanted to know in what, exactly, this Negro-African culture consisted and, more, why it was judged necessary to save it. He ended, somewhat vaguely, by saying that, in his opinion, it was human values which had to be preserved, human needs which had to be respected and expressed.

This admirable but quite inadequate psychologist precipitated something of a storm. Diop tried to answer the first part of his question by pointing out that, in their attitudes toward their cultures, a great diversity of viewpoints also obtained among black men. Then an enormous, handsome, extremely impressive black man whom I had not remarked before, who was also

named Cesaire, stated that the contemporary crisis of
black cultures had been brought about by Europe's nine-
teenth- and twentieth-century attempts to impose their
culture on other peoples. They did this without any
recognition of the cultural validity of these peoples and
thus aroused their resistance. In the case of Africa,
where culture was fluid and largely unwritten, resistance
had been most difficult. "Which is why," he said, "we
are here. We are the most characteristic products of this
crisis." And then a rage seemed to shake him, and he
continued in a voice thick with fury, "Nothing will ever
make us believe that our beliefs . . . are merely frivolous
superstitions. No power will ever cause us to admit that
we are lower than any other people." He then made a
reference to the present Arab struggle against the French
which I did not understand, and ended, "What we are
doing is holding on to what is ours. Little," he added,
sardonically, "but it belongs to us."

Aimé Cesaire, to whom the question had been addressed, was finally able to answer it. He pointed out,
with a deliberate, mocking logic, that the rejection by a
European of European culture was of the utmost unim-
portance. "Reject it or not, he is still a European, even
his rejection is a European rejection. We do not choose
our cultures, we belong to them." As to the speaker's implied idea of cultural relativity, and the progressive role
this idea can sometimes play, he cited the French objection to this idea. It is an idea which, by making all cul-

tures, as such, equal, undermines French justification for its presence in Africa. He also suggested that the speaker had implied that this conference was primarily interested in an idealistic reconstruction of the past. "But our attitude," said Cesaire, "toward colonialism and racial discrimination is very concrete. Our aims cannot be realized without this concreteness." And as for the question of race: "No one is suggesting that there is such a thing as a pure race, or that culture is a racial product. We are not Negroes by our own desire, but, in effect, because of Europe. What unites all Negroes is the injustices they have suffered at European hands."

The moment Cesaire finished, Cheik Anta Diop passionately demanded if it were a heresy from a Marxist point of view to try to hang onto a national culture. "Where," he asked, "is the European nation which, in order to progress, surrendered its past?"

There was no answer to this question, nor were there any further questions from the audience. Richard Wright spoke briefly, saying that this conference marked a turning point in the history of Euro-African relations: it marked, in fact, the beginning of the end of the European domination. He spoke of the great diversity of techniques and approaches now at the command of black people, with particular emphasis on the role the American Negro could be expected to play. Among black people, the American Negro was in the technological vanguard and this could prove of inestimable value to the developing African sovereignties. And the dialogue ended immediately afterward, at six-fifty-five, with Senghor's statement that this was the first of many such conferences, the first of many dialogues. As night was falling we poured into the Paris streets. Boys and girls, old men and women, bicycles, terraces, all were there, and the people were queueing up before the bakeries for bread.

3. Fifth Avenue, Uptown:

A Letter from Harlem

THERE IS A HOUSING PROJECT standing now where the house in which we grew up once stood, and one of those stunted city trees is snarling where our doorway used to be. This is on the rehabilitated side of the avenue. The other side of the avenue—for progress takes time—has not been rehabilitated yet and it looks exactly as it looked in the days when we sat with our noses pressed against the windowpane, longing to be allowed to go "across the street." The grocery store which gave us credit is still there, and there can be no doubt that it is still giving credit. The people in the project certainly need it—far more, indeed, than they ever needed the project. The last time I passed by, the Jewish proprietor was still standing among his shelves, looking sadder and heavier but scarcely any older. Farther down the block stands the shoe-repair store in which our shoes were repaired until reparation became impossible and in which, then, we bought all our "new" ones. The Negro proprietor is still in the window, head down, working at the leather.

These two, I imagine, could tell a long tale if they would (perhaps they would be glad to if they could), having watched so many, for so long, struggling in the fishhooks, the barbed wire, of this avenue.

The avenue is elsewhere the renowned and elegant Fifth. The area I am describing, which, in today's gang parlance, would be called "the turf," is bounded by Lenox Avenue on the west, the Harlem River on the east, 135th Street on the north, and 130th Street on the south. We never lived beyond these boundaries; this is where we grew up. Walking along 145th Street—for example —familiar as it is, and similar, does not have the same impact because I do not know any of the people on the block. But when I turn east on 131st Street and Lenox Avenue, there is first a soda-pop joint, then a shoeshine "parlor," then a grocery store, then a dry cleaners', then the houses. All along the street there are people who watched me grow up, people who grew up with me, people I watched grow up along with my brothers and sisters; and, sometimes in my arms, sometimes underfoot, sometimes at my shoulder—or on it—their children, a riot, a forest of children, who include my nieces and nephews.

When we reach the end of this long block, we find

ourselves on wide, filthy, hostile Fifth Avenue, facing
that project which hangs over the avenue like a monu-
ment to the folly, and the cowardice, of good intentions.
All along the block, for anyone who knows it, are immense human gaps, like craters. These gaps are not
created merely by those who have moved away, inevitably into some other ghetto; or by those who have risen,
almost always into a greater capacity for self-loathing
and self-delusion; or yet by those who, by whatever
means—War II, the Korean war, a policeman's gun or
billy, a gang war, a brawl, madness, an overdose of
heroin, or, simply, unnatural exhaustion—are dead. I
am talking about those who are left, and I am talking
principally about the young. What are they doing? Well,
some, a minority, are fanatical churchgoers, members of
the more extreme of the Holy Roller sects. Many, many
more are "moslems," by affiliation or sympathy, that is
to say that they are united by nothing more—and nothing less—than a hatred of the white world and all its
works. They are present, for example, at every Buy
Black street-corner meeting—meetings in which the
speaker urges his hearers to cease trading with white
men and establish a separate economy. Neither the
speaker nor his hearers can possibly do this, of course,
since Negroes do not own General Motors or RCA or
the A & P, nor, indeed, do they own more than a wholly
insufficient fraction of anything else in Harlem (those
who *do* own anything are more interested in their profits

than in their fellows). But these meetings nevertheless keep alive in the participators a certain pride of bitterness without which, however futile this bitterness may be, they could scarcely remain alive at all. Many have given up. They stay home and watch the TV screen, living on the earnings of their parents, cousins, brothers, or uncles, and only leave the house to go to the movies or to the nearest bar. "How're you making it?" one may ask, running into them along the block, or in the bar. "Oh, I'm TV-ing it"; with the saddest, sweetest, most shamefaced of smiles, and from a great distance. This distance one is compelled to respect; anyone who has traveled so far will not easily be dragged again into the world. There are further retreats, of course, than the TV screen or the bar. There are those who are simply sitting on their stoops, "stoned," animated for a moment only, and hideously, by the approach of someone who may lend them the money for a "fix." Or by the approach of someone from whom they can purchase it, one of the shrewd ones, on the way to prison or just coming out.

And the others, who have avoided all of these deaths, get up in the morning and go downtown to meet "the man." They work in the white man's world all day and come home in the evening to this fetid block. They struggle to instill in their children some private sense of honor or dignity which will help the child to survive. This means, of course, that they must struggle, stolidly, incessantly, to keep this sense alive in themselves, in

spite of the insults, the indifference, and the cruelty
they are certain to encounter in their working day. They
patiently browbeat the landlord into fixing the heat, the
plaster, the plumbing; this demands prodigious patience; nor is patience usually enough. In trying to make
their hovels habitable, they are perpetually throwing
good money after bad. Such frustration, so long endured, is driving many strong, admirable men and
women whose only crime is color to the very gates of
paranoia.

One remembers them from another time—playing
handball in the playground, going to church, wondering
if they were going to be promoted at school. One remembers them going off to war—gladly, to escape this block.
One remembers their return. Perhaps one remembers
their wedding day. And one sees where the girl is now
—vainly looking for salvation from some other embittered, trussed, and struggling boy—and sees the all-but-
abandoned children in the streets.

Now I am perfectly aware that there are other slums
in which white men are fighting for their lives, and
mainly losing. I know that blood is also flowing through
those streets and that the human damage there is incalculable. People are continually pointing out to me
the wretchedness of white people in order to console me
for the wretchedness of blacks. But an itemized account
of the American failure does not console me and it
should not console anyone else. That hundreds of thou-

sands of white people are living, in effect, no better than the "niggers" is not a fact to be regarded with complacency. The social and moral bankruptcy suggested by this fact is of the bitterest, most terrifying kind.

The people, however, who believe that this democratic anguish has some consoling value are always pointing out that So-and-So, white, and So-and-So, black, rose from the slums into the big time. The existence—the public existence—of, say, Frank Sinatra and Sammy Davis, Jr. proves to them that America is still the land of opportunity and that inequalities vanish before the determined will. It proves nothing of the sort. The determined will is rare—at the moment, in this country, it is unspeakably rare—and the inequalities suffered by the many are in no way justified by the rise of a few. A few have always risen—in every country, every era, and in the teeth of regimes which can by no stretch of the imagination be thought of as free. Not all of these people, it is worth remembering, left the world better than they found it. The determined will is rare, but it is not invariably benevolent. Furthermore, the American equation of success with the big times reveals an awful disrespect for human life and human achievement. This equation has placed our cities among the most dangerous in the world and has placed our youth among the most empty and most bewildered. The situation of our youth is not mysterious. Children have never been very good at listening to their elders, but they have never failed to imitate them. They must, they have no other models. That is exactly what our children are doing. They are imitating our immorality, our disrespect for the pain of others.

All other slum dwellers, when the bank account permits it, can move out of the slum and vanish altogether from the eye of persecution. No Negro in this country has ever made that much money and it will be a long time before any Negro does. The Negroes in Harlem, who have no money, spend what they have on such gimcracks as they are sold. These include "wider" TV screens, more "faithful" hi-fi sets, more "powerful" cars, all of which, of course, are obsolete long before they are paid for. Anyone who has ever struggled with poverty knows how extremely expensive it is to be poor; and if one is a member of a captive population, economically speaking, one's feet have simply been placed on the treadmill forever. One is victimized, economically, in a thousand ways—rent, for example, or car insurance. Go shopping one day in Harlem—for anything—and compare Harlem prices and quality with those downtown.

The people who have managed to get off this block have only got as far as a more respectable ghetto. This respectable ghetto does not even have the advantages of the disreputable one—friends, neighbors, a familiar church, and friendly tradesmen; and it is not, moreover, in the nature of any ghetto to remain respectable long.

Every Sunday, people who have left the block take the
lonely ride back, dragging their increasingly discon-
tented children with them. They spend the day talking,
not always with words, about the trouble they've seen
and the trouble—one must watch their eyes as they
watch their children—they are only too likely to see.
For children do not like ghettos. It takes them nearly no
time to discover exactly why they are there.

The projects in Harlem are hated. They are hated almost as much as policemen, and this is saying a great
deal. And they are hated for the same reason: both reveal, unbearably, the real attitude of the white world, no
matter how many liberal speeches are made, no matter
how many lofty editorials are written, no matter how
many civil-rights commissions are set up.

The projects are hideous, of course, there being a law,
apparently respected throughout the world, that popular
housing shall be as cheerless as a prison. They are
lumped all over Harlem, colorless, bleak, high, and re-
volting. The wide windows look out on Harlem's in-
vincible and indescribable squalor: the Park Avenue
railroad tracks, around which, about forty years ago, the
present dark community began; the unrehabilitated
houses, bowed down, it would seem, under the great
weight of frustration and bitterness they contain; the
dark, the ominous schoolhouses from which the child
may emerge maimed, blinded, hooked, or enraged for

life; and the churches, churches, block upon block of churches, niched in the walls like cannon in the walls of a fortress. Even if the administration of the projects were not so insanely humiliating (for example: one must report raises in salary to the management, which will then eat up the profit by raising one's rent; the management has the right to know who is staying in your apartment; the management can ask you to leave, at their discretion), the projects would still be hated because they are an insult to the meanest intelligence.

Harlem got its first private project, Riverton*—which is now, naturally, a slum—about twelve years ago because at that time Negroes were not allowed to live in Stuyvesant Town. Harlem watched Riverton go up, therefore, in the most violent bitterness of spirit, and hated it long before the builders arrived. They began hating it at about the time people began moving out of their condemned houses to make room for this additional proof of how thoroughly the white world despised them. And they had scarcely moved in, naturally, before

* The inhabitants of Riverton were much embittered by this description; they have, apparently, forgotten how their project came into being; and have repeatedly informed me that I cannot possibly be referring to Riverton, but to another housing project which is directly across the street. It is quite clear, I think, that I have no interest in accusing any individuals or families of the depredations herein described: but neither can I deny the evidence of my own eyes. Nor do I blame anyone in Harlem for making the best of a dreadful bargain. But anyone who lives in Harlem and imagines that he has *not* struck this bargain, or that what he takes to be his status (in whose eyes?) protects him against the common pain, demoralization, and danger, is simply self deluded.

they began smashing windows, defacing walls, urinating in the elevators, and fornicating in the playgrounds. Liberals, both white and black, were appalled at the spectacle. I was appalled by the liberal innocence—or cynicism, which comes out in practice as much the same thing. Other people were delighted to be able to point to proof positive that nothing could be done to better the lot of the colored people. They were, and are, right in one respect: that nothing can be done as long as they are treated like colored people. The people in Harlem know they are living there because white people do not think they are good enough to live anywhere else. No amount of "improvement" can sweeten this fact. Whatever money is now being earmarked to improve this, or any other ghetto, might as well be burnt. A ghetto can be improved in one way only: out of existence.

Similarly, the only way to police a ghetto is to be oppressive. None of the Police Commissioner's men, even with the best will in the world, have any way of understanding the lives led by the people they swagger about in twos and threes controlling. Their very presence is an insult, and it would be, even if they spent their entire day feeding gumdrops to children. They represent the force of the white world, and that world's real intentions are, simply, for that world's criminal profit and ease, to keep the black man corraled up here, in his place. The badge, the gun in the holster, and the swinging club make vivid what will happen should his rebellion become overt. Rare, indeed, is the Harlem citizen, from the most circumspect church member to the most shiftless adolescent, who does not have a long tale to tell of police incompetence, injustice, or brutality. I myself have witnessed and endured it more than once. The businessmen and racketeers also have a story. And so do the prostitutes. (And this is not, perhaps, the place to discuss Harlem's very complex attitude toward black policemen, nor the reasons, according to Harlem, that they are nearly all downtown.)

It is hard, on the other hand, to blame the policeman, blank, good-natured, thoughtless, and insuperably innocent, for being such a perfect representative of the people he serves. He, too, believes in good intentions and is astounded and offended when they are not taken for the deed. He has never, himself, done anything for which to be hated—which of us has?—and yet he is facing, daily and nightly, people who would gladly see him dead, and he knows it. There is no way for him not to know it: there are few things under heaven more unnerving than the silent, accumulating contempt and hatred of a people. He moves through Harlem, therefore, like an occupying soldier in a bitterly hostile country; which is precisely what, and where, he is, and is the reason he walks in twos and threes. And he is not the only one who knows why he is always in company: the people who are watching him know why, too. Any street meeting, sacred or secular, which he and his colleagues uneasily cover has as its explicit or implicit burden the cruelty and injustice of the white domination. And these days, of course, in terms increasingly vivid and jubilant, it speaks of the end of that domination. The white policeman standing on a Harlem street corner finds himself at the very center of the revolution now occurring in the world. He is not prepared for it—naturally, nobody is —and, what is possibly much more to the point, he is exposed, as few white people are, to the anguish of the black people around him. Even if he is gifted with the merest mustard grain of imagination, something must seep in. He cannot avoid observing that some of the children, in spite of their color, remind him of children he has known and loved, perhaps even of his own children. He knows that he certainly does not want *his* children living this way. He can retreat from his uneasiness in only one direction: into a callousness which very shortly becomes second nature. He becomes more callous, the population becomes more hostile, the situation grows more tense, and the police force is increased. One day, to everyone's astonishment, someone drops a match in the powder keg and everything blows up. Before the dust has settled or the blood congealed, editorials, speeches, and civil-rights commissions are loud in the land, demanding to know what happened. What happened is that Negroes want to be treated like men.

Negroes want to be treated like men: a perfectly straightforward statement, containing only seven words.

People who have mastered Kant, Hegel, Shakespeare, Marx, Freud, and the Bible find this statement utterly impenetrable. The idea seems to threaten profound, barely conscious assumptions. A kind of panic paralyzes their features, as though they found themselves trapped on the edge of a steep place. I once tried to describe to a very well-known American intellectual the conditions among Negroes in the South. My recital disturbed him and made him indignant; and he asked me in perfect innocence, "Why don't all the Negroes in the South move North?" I tried to explain what *has* happened, unfailingly, whenever a significant body of Negroes move North. They do not escape Jim Crow: they merely encounter another, not-less-deadly variety. They do not move to Chicago, they move to the South Side; they do not move to New York, they move to Harlem. The pressure within the ghetto causes the ghetto walls to expand, and this expansion is always violent. White people hold the line as long as they can, and in as many ways as they can, from verbal intimidation to physical violence. But inevitably the border which has divided the ghetto from the rest of the world falls into the hands of the ghetto. The white people fall back bitterly before the black horde; the landlords make a tidy profit by raising the rent, chopping up the rooms, and all but dispensing with the upkeep; and what has once been a neighborhood turns into a "turf." This is precisely what happened when the Puerto Ricans arrived in their thousands—and the bitterness thus caused is, as I write, being fought out all up and down those streets.

Northerners indulge in an extremely dangerous luxury. They seem to feel that because they fought on the right side during the Civil War, and won, they have earned the right merely to deplore what is going on in the South, without taking any responsibility for it; and that they can ignore what is happening in Northern cities because what is happening in Little Rock or Birmingham is worse. Well, in the first place, it is not possible for anyone who has not endured both to know which is "worse." I know Negroes who prefer the South and white Southerners, because "At least there, you haven't got to play any guessing games!" The guessing games referred to have driven more than one Negro into the narcotics ward, the madhouse, or the river. I know another Negro, a man very dear to me, who says, with conviction and with truth, "The spirit of the South is the spirit of America." He was born in the North and did his military training in the South. He did not, as far as I can gather, find the South "worse"; he found it, if anything, all too familiar. In the second place, though, even if Birmingham *is* worse, no doubt Johannesburg, South Africa, beats it by several miles, and Buchenwald was one of the worst things that ever happened in the entire history of the world. The world has never lacked for horrifying examples; but I do not believe that these examples are meant to be used as justification for our own crimes. This perpetual justification empties the heart of all human feeling. The emptier our hearts become, the greater will be our crimes. Thirdly, the South is not merely an embarrassingly backward region, but a part of this country, and what happens there concerns every one of us.

As far as the color problem is concerned, there is but one great difference between the Southern white and the Northerner: the Southerner remembers, historically and in his own psyche, a kind of Eden in which he loved black people and they loved him. Historically, the flaming sword laid across this Eden is the Civil War. Personally, it is the Southerner's sexual coming of age, when, without any warning, unbreakable taboos are set up between himself and his past. Everything, thereafter, is permitted him except the love he remembers and has never ceased to need. The resulting, indescribable torment affects every Southern mind and is the basis of the Southern hysteria.

None of this is true for the Northerner. Negroes represent nothing to him personally, except, perhaps, the dangers of carnality. He never sees Negroes. Southerners see them all the time. Northerners never think about them whereas Southerners are never really thinking of anything else. Negroes are, therefore, ignored in the North and are under surveillance in the South, and suffer hideously in both places. Neither the Southerner nor the Northerner is able to look on the Negro simply as a man. It seems to be indispensable to the national self-esteem that the Negro be considered either as a kind of ward (in which case we are told how many Negroes, comparatively, bought Cadillacs last year and how few, comparatively, were lynched), or as a victim (in which case we are promised that he will never vote in our assemblies or go to school with our kids). They are two sides of the same coin and the South will not change— *cannot* change—until the North changes. The country will not change until it re-examines itself and discovers what it really means by freedom. In the meantime, generations keep being born, bitterness is increased by incompetence, pride, and folly, and the world shrinks around us.

It is a terrible, an inexorable, law that one cannot deny the humanity of another without diminishing one's own: in the face of one's victim, one sees oneself. Walk through the streets of Harlem and see what we, this nation, have become.

4. East River, Downtown:

Postscript to a Letter from Harlem

THE FACT THAT AMERICAN NE-
groes rioted in the U.N. while Adlai Stevenson was
addressing the Assembly shocked and baffled most white
Americans. Stevenson's speech, and the spectacular disturbance in the gallery, were both touched off by the
death, in Katanga, the day before, of Patrice Lumumba.
Stevenson stated, in the course of his address, that the
United States was "against" colonialism. God knows
what the African nations, who hold 25 per cent
of the voting stock in the U.N. were thinking—they
may, for example, have been thinking of the U.S. ab-
stention when the vote on Algerian freedom was before
the Assembly—but I think I have a fairly accurate notion of what the Negroes in the gallery were thinking.
I had intended to be there myself. It was my first reaction upon hearing of Lumumba's death. I was curious
about the impact of this political assassination on Ne-

groes in Harlem, for Lumumba had—has—captured
the popular imagination there. I was curious to know if
Lumumba's death, which is surely among the most sinister of recent events, would elicit from "our" side anything more than the usual, well-meaning rhetoric. And I
was curious about the African reaction.

However, the chaos on my desk prevented my being
in the U.N. gallery. Had I been there, I, too, in the eyes
of most Americans, would have been merely a pawn in
the hands of the Communists. The climate and the events
of the last decade, and the steady pressure of the "cold"
war, have given Americans yet another means of avoiding self-examination, and so it has been decided that the
riots were "Communist" inspired. Nor was it long, naturally, before prominent Negroes rushed forward to as-
sure the republic that the U.N. rioters do not represent
the real feeling of the Negro community.

According, then, to what I take to be the prevailing
view, these rioters were merely a handful of irrespon-
sible, Stalinist-corrupted *provocateurs*.

I find this view amazing. It is a view which even a
minimal effort at observation would immediately con-
tradict. One has only, for example, to walk through
Harlem and ask oneself two questions. The first question
is: Would *I* like to live here? And the second question is:
Why don't those who now live here move out? The answer to both questions is immediately obvious. Unless
one takes refuge in the theory—however disguised—
that Negroes are, somehow, different from white peo-

ple, I do not see how one can escape the conclusion that the Negro's status in this country is not only a cruel injustice but a grave national liability.

Now, I do not doubt that, among the people at the U.N. that day, there were Stalinist and professional revolutionists acting out of the most cynical motives. Wherever there is great social discontent, these people are, sooner or later, to be found. Their presence is not as frightening as the discontent which creates their opportunity. What I find appalling—and really dangerous— is the American assumption that the Negro is so contented with his lot here that only the cynical agents of a foreign power can rouse him to protest. It is a notion which contains a gratuitous insult, implying, as it does, that Negroes can make no move unless they are manipulated. It forcibly suggests that the Southern attitude toward the Negro is also, essentially, the national attitude. When the South has trouble with its Negroes— when the Negroes refuse to remain in their "place"— it blames "outside" agitators and "Northern interference." When the nation has trouble with the Northern Negro, it blames the Kremlin. And this, by no means incidentally, is a very dangerous thing to do. We thus give credit to the Communists for attitudes and victories which are not theirs. We make of them the champions of the oppressed, and they could not, of course, be more delighted.

If, as is only too likely, one prefers not to visit Har-

lem and expose oneself to the anguish there, one has
only to consider the two most powerful movements
among Negroes in this country today. At one pole, there
is the Negro student movement. This movement, I believe, will prove to be the very last attempt made by
American Negroes to achieve acceptance in the republic,
to force the country to honor its own ideals. The movement does not have as its goal the consumption of over-
cooked hamburgers and tasteless coffee at various sleazy
lunch counters. Neither do Negroes, who have, largely,
been produced by miscegenation, share the white man's
helplessly hypocritical attitudes toward the time-honored
and universal mingling. The goal of the student movement is nothing less than the liberation of the entire country from its most crippling attitudes and habits. The reason that it is important—of the utmost importance—for
white people, here, to see the Negroes as people like
themselves is that white people will not, otherwise, be
able to see themselves as they are.

At the other pole is the Muslim movement, which
daily becomes more powerful. The Muslims do not expect anything at all from the white people of this country. They do not believe that the American professions
of democracy or equality have ever been even remotely
sincere. They insist on the total separation of the races.
This is to be achieved by the acquisition of land from
the United States—land which is owed the Negroes as
"back wages" for the labor wrested from them when

they were slaves, and for their unrecognized and unhon-
ored contributions to the wealth and power of this country. The student movement depends, at bottom, on an
act of faith, an ability to see, beneath the cruelty and
hysteria and apathy of white people, their bafflement
and pain and essential decency. This is superbly difficult. It demands a perpetually cultivated spiritual resili-
ence, for the bulk of the evidence contradicts the vision.
But the Muslim movement has all the evidence on its
side. Unless one supposes that the idea of black su-
premacy has virtues denied to the idea of white suprem-
acy, one cannot possibly accept the deadly conclusions a
Muslim draws from this evidence. On the other hand, it
is quite impossible to argue with a Muslim concerning
the actual state of Negroes in this country—the truth,
after all, is the truth.

This is the great power a Muslim speaker has over
his audience. His audience has not heard this truth—
the truth about their daily lives—honored by anyone
else. Almost anyone else, black or white, prefers to
soften this truth, and point to a new day which is coming in America. But this day has been coming for nearly
one hundred years. Viewed solely in the light of this
country's moral professions, this lapse is inexcusable.
Even more important, however, is the fact that there is
desperately little in the record to indicate that white
America ever seriously desired—or desires—to see this
day arrive.

Usually, for example, those white people who are in favor of integration prove to be in favor of it later, in some other city, some other town, some other building, some other school. The arguments, or rationalizations, with which they attempt to disguise their panic cannot be respected. Northerners proffer their indignation about the South as a kind of badge, as proof of good intentions; never suspecting that they thus increase, in the heart of the Negro they are speaking to, a kind of helpless pain and rage—and pity. Negroes know how little most white people are prepared to implement their words with deeds, how little, when the chips are down, they are prepared to risk. And this long history of moral evasion has had an unhealthy effect on the total life of the country, and has eroded whatever respect Negroes may once have felt for white people.

We are beginning, therefore, to witness in this country a new thing. "I am not at all sure," states one prominent Negro, who is *not* a Muslim, "that I *want* to be integrated into a burning house." "I might," says another, "consider being integrated into something else, an American society more real and more honest—but *this?* No, thank you, man, who *needs* it?" And this searching disaffection has everything to do with the emergence of Africa: "At the rate things are going here, all of Africa will be free before we can get a lousy cup of coffee."

Now, of course, it is easy to say—and it is true

enough, as far as it goes—that the American Negro deludes himself if he imagines himself capable of any loyalty other than his loyalty to the United States. He is an American, too, and he will survive or perish with the country. This seems an unanswerable argument. But, while I have no wish whatever to question the loyalty of American Negroes, I think this argument may be examined with some profit. The argument is used, I think, too often and too glibly. It obscures the effects of the passage of time, and the great changes that have taken place in the world.

In the first place, as the homeless wanderers of the twentieth century prove, the question of nationality no longer necessarily involves the question of allegiance. Allegiance, after all, has to work two ways; and one can grow weary of an allegiance which is not reciprocal. I have the right and the duty, for example, in my country, to vote; but it is my country's responsibility to protect my right to vote. People now approaching, or past, middle age, who have spent their lives in such struggles, have thereby acquired an understanding of America, and a belief in her potential which cannot now be shaken. (There are exceptions to this, however, W. E. B. Du Bois, for example. It is easy to dismiss him as a Stalinist; but it is more interesting to consider just why so intelligent a man became so disillusioned.) But I very strongly doubt that any Negro youth, now approaching maturity, and with the whole, vast world

before him, is willing, say, to settle for Jim Crow in
Miami, when he can—or, before the travel ban, *could*
—feast at the welcome table in Havana. And he need
not, to prefer Havana, have any pro-Communist, or, for
that matter, pro-Cuban, or pro-Castro sympathies: he
need merely prefer not to be treated as a second-class
citizen.

These are extremely unattractive facts, but they *are*
facts, and no purpose is served by denying them. Neither,
as I have already tried to indicate, is any purpose served
by pretending that Negroes who refuse to be bound by
this country's peculiar attitudes are subversive. They
have every right to refuse to be bound by a set of attitudes as useless now and as obsolete as the pillory.
Finally, the time is forever behind us when Negroes
could be expected to "wait." What is demanded now,
and at once, is not that Negroes continue to adjust themselves to the cruel racial pressures of life in the United
States but that the United States readjust itself to the
facts of life in the present world.

One of these facts is that the American Negro can no
longer, nor will he ever again, be controlled by white
America's image of him. This fact has everything to do
with the rise of Africa in world affairs. At the time that
I was growing up, Negroes in this country were taught
to be ashamed of Africa. They were taught it bluntly, as
I was, for example, by being told that Africa had never
contributed "anything" to civilization. Or one was taught

the same lesson more obliquely, and even more effec-
tively, by watching nearly naked, dancing, comic-opera,
cannibalistic savages in the movies. They were nearly
always all bad, sometimes funny, sometimes both. If
one of them was good, his goodness was proved by his
loyalty to the white man. A baffling sort of goodness,
particularly as one's father, who certainly wanted one to
be "good," was more than likely to come home cursing
—cursing the white man. One's hair was always being
attacked with hard brushes and combs and Vaseline: it
was shameful to have "nappy" hair. One's legs and
arms and face were always being greased, so that one
would not look "ashy" in the wintertime. One was always being mercilessly scrubbed and polished, as though
in the hope that a stain could thus be washed away—I
hazard that the Negro children of my generation, anyway, had an earlier and more painful acquaintance with
soap than any other children anywhere. The women were
forever straightening and curling their hair, and using
bleaching creams. And yet it was clear that none of this
effort would release one from the stigma and danger of
being a Negro; this effort merely increased the shame
and rage. There was not, no matter where one turned,
any acceptable image of oneself, no proof of one's existence. One had the choice, either of "acting just like a
nigger" or of *not* acting just like a nigger—and only
those who have tried it know how impossible it is to tell
the difference.

My first hero was Joe Louis. I was ashamed of Father Divine. Haile Selassie was the first black emperor I ever saw—in a newsreel; he was pleading vainly with the West to prevent the rape of his country. And the extraordinary complex of tensions thus set up in the breast, between hatred of whites and contempt for blacks, is very hard to describe. Some of the most energetic people of my generation were destroyed by this interior warfare.

But none of this is so for those who are young now. The power of the white world to control their identities was crumbling as they were born; and by the time they were able to react to the world, Africa was on the stage of history. This could not but have an extraordinary effect on their own morale, for it meant that they were not merely the descendants of slaves in a white, Protestant, and puritan country: they were also related to kings and princes in an ancestral homeland, far away. And this has proved to be a great antidote to the poison of self-hatred.

It also signals, at last, the end of the Negro situation in this country, as we have so far known it. Any effort, from here on out, to keep the Negro in his "place" can only have the most extreme and unlucky repercussions. This being so, it would seem to me that the most intelligent effort we can now make is to give up this doomed endeavor and study how we can most quickly end this division in our house. The Negroes who rioted in the

U.N. are but a very small echo of the black discontent now abroad in the world. If we are not able, and quickly, to face and begin to eliminate the sources of this discontent in our own country, we will never be able to do it on the great stage of the world.

5. A Fly in Buttermilk

You CAN TAKE THE CHILD OUT of the country," my elders were fond of saying, "but you can't take the country out of the child." They were speaking of their own antecedents, I supposed; it didn't, anyway, seem possible that they could be warning me; I took myself out of the country and went to Paris. It was there I discovered that the old folks knew what they had been talking about: I found myself, willy-nilly, alchemized into an American the moment I touched French soil.

Now, back again after nearly nine years, it was ironical to reflect that if I had not lived in France for so long I would never have found it necessary—or possible—to visit the American South. The South had always frightened me. How deeply it had frightened me —though I had never seen it—and how soon, was one of the things my dreams revealed to me while I was there. And this made me think of the privacy and mystery of childhood all over again, in a new way. I wondered where children got their strength—the strength, in this case, to walk through mobs to get to school.

"You've got to remember," said an older Negro friend to me, in Washington, "that no matter what you see or how it makes you feel, it can't be compared to twenty-five, thirty years ago—you remember those photographs of Negroes hanging from trees?" I looked at him differently. *I* had seen the photographs—but *he* might have been one of them. "I remember," he said, "when conductors on streetcars wore pistols and had police powers." And he remembered a great deal more. He remembered, for example, hearing Booker T. Washington speak, and the day-to-day progress of the Scottsboro case, and the rise and bloody fall of Bessie Smith. These had been books and headlines and music for me but it now developed that they were also a part of my identity.

"You're just one generation away from the South, you know. You'll find," he added, kindly, "that people will be willing to talk to you . . . if they don't feel that you look down on them just because you're from the North."

The first Negro I encountered, an educator, didn't give me any opportunity to look down. He forced me to admit, at once, that I had never been to college; that Northern Negroes lived herded together, like pigs

in a pen; that the campus on which we met was a tribute
to the industry and determination of Southern Negroes.
"Negroes in the South form a *community*." My humilia-
tion was complete with his discovery that I couldn't
even drive a car. I couldn't ask him anything. He made
me feel so hopeless an example of the general Northern
spinelessness that it would have seemed a spiteful coun-
terattack to have asked him to discuss the integration
problem which had placed his city in the headlines.

At the same time, I felt that there was nothing which
bothered him more; but perhaps he did not really
know what he thought about it; or thought too many
things at once. His campus risked being very different
twenty years from now. Its special function would be
gone—and so would his position, arrived at with such
pain. The new day a-coming was not for him. I don't
think this fact made him bitter but I think it frightened him and made him sad; for the future is like
heaven—everyone exalts it but no one wants to go there
now. And I imagine that he shared the attitude, which
I was to encounter so often later, toward the children
who were helping to bring this future about: admiration
before the general spectacle and skepticism before the
individual case.

That evening I went to visit G., one of the "integrated"
children, a boy of about fifteen. I had already heard
something of his first day in school, the peculiar prob-

lems his presence caused, and his own extraordinary
bearing.

He seemed extraordinary at first mainly by his silence. He was tall for his age and, typically, seemed
to be constructed mainly of sharp angles, such as
elbows and knees. Dark gingerbread sort of coloring,
with ordinary hair, and a face disquietingly impassive,
save for his very dark, very large eyes. I got the impression, each time that he raised them, not so much
that they spoke but that they registered volumes; each
time he dropped them it was as though he had retired
into the library.

We sat in the living room, his mother, younger
brother and sister, and I, while G. sat on the sofa, doing
his homework. The father was at work and the older
sister had not yet come home. The boy had looked up
once, as I came in, to say, "Good evening, sir," and
then left all the rest to his mother.

Mrs. R. was a very strong-willed woman, handsome,
quiet-looking, dressed in black. Nothing, she told me,
beyond name-calling, had marked G.'s first day at
school; but on the second day she received the last of
several threatening phone calls. She was told that if she
didn't want her son "cut to ribbons" she had better
keep him at home. She heeded this warning to the
extent of calling the chief of police.

"He told me to go on and send him. He said he'd
be there when the cutting started. So I sent him." Even
more remarkably perhaps, G. went.

No one cut him, in fact no one touched him. The students formed a wall between G. and the entrances, saying only enough, apparently, to make their intention clearly understood, watching him, and keeping him outside. (I asked him, "What did you feel when they blocked your way?" G. looked up at me, very briefly, with no expression on his face, and told me, "Nothing, sir.") At last the principal appeared and took him by the hand and they entered the school, while the children shouted behind them, "Nigger-lover!"

G. was alone all day at school.

"But I thought you already knew some of the kids there," I said. I had been told that he had friends among the white students because of their previous competition in a Soapbox Derby.

"Well, none of them are in his classes," his mother told me—a shade too quickly, as though she did not want to dwell on the idea of G.'s daily isolation.

"We don't have the same schedule," G. said. It was as though he were coming to his mother's rescue. Then, unwillingly, with a kind of interior shrug, "Some of the guys had lunch with me but then the other kids called them names." He went back to his homework.

I began to realize that there were not only a great many things G. would not tell me, there was much that he would never tell his mother.

"But nobody bothers you, anyway?"

"No," he said. "They just—call names. I don't let it bother me."

Nevertheless, the principal frequently escorts him through the halls. One day, when G. was alone, a boy tripped him and knocked him down and G. reported this to the principal. The white boy denied it but a few days later, while G. and the principal were together, he came over and said, "I'm sorry I tripped you; I won't do it again," and they shook hands. But it doesn't seem that this boy has as yet developed into a friend. And it is clear that G. will not allow himself to expect this.

I asked Mrs. R. what had prompted her to have her son reassigned to a previously all-white high school. She sighed, paused; then, sharply, "Well, it's not because I'm so anxious to have him around white people." Then she laughed. "I really don't know how I'd feel if I was to carry a white baby around who was calling me Grandma." G. laughed, too, for the first time. "White people say," the mother went on, "that that's all a Negro wants. I don't think they believe that themselves."

Then we switched from the mysterious question of what white folks believe to the relatively solid ground of what she, herself, knows and fears.

"You see that boy? Well, he's always been a straight-A student. He didn't hardly have to work at it. You see the way he's so quiet now on the sofa, with his books? Well, when he was going to ———— High School, he didn't have no homework or if he did, he could get it done in five minutes. Then, there he was, out in the streets, getting into mischief, and all he did all day in school was just keep clowning to make the other boys laugh. He wasn't learning nothing and didn't nobody care if he *never* learned nothing and I could just see what was going to happen to him if he kept on like that."

The boy was very quiet.

"What were you learning in ——— High?" I asked him.

"Nothing!" he exploded, with a very un-boyish laugh. I asked him to tell me about it.

"Well, the teacher comes in," he said, "and she gives you something to read and she goes out. She leaves some other student in charge . . ." ("You can just imagine how much reading gets done," Mrs. R. interposed.) "At the end of the period," G. continued, "she comes back and tells you something to read for the next day."

So, having nothing else to do, G. began amusing his classmates and his mother began to be afraid. G. is just about at the age when boys begin dropping out of school. Perhaps they get a girl into trouble; she also drops out; the boy gets work for a time or gets into trouble for a long time. I was told that forty-five girls had left school for the maternity ward the year before. A week or ten days before I arrived in the city eighteen boys from G.'s former high school had been sentenced to the chain gang.

"My boy's a good boy," said Mrs. R., "and I wanted to see him have a chance."

"Don't the teachers care about the students?" I

asked. This brought forth more laughter. How could
they care? How much could they do if they *did* care?
There were too many children, from shaky homes and
worn-out parents, in aging, inadequate plants. They
could be considered, most of them, as already doomed.
Besides, the teachers' jobs were safe. They were responsible only to the principal, an appointed official, whose
judgment, apparently, was never questioned by his
(white) superiors or confreres.

The principal of G.'s former high school was about
seventy-five when he was finally retired and his idea
of discipline was to have two boys beat each other—
"under his supervision"—with leather belts. This once
happened with G., with no other results than that his
parents gave the principal a tongue-lashing. It happened with two boys of G.'s acquaintance with the result that, after school, one boy beat the other so badly
that he had to be sent to the hospital. The teachers have
themselves arrived at a dead end, for in a segregated
school system they cannot rise any higher, and the
students are aware of this. Both students and teachers
soon cease to struggle.

"If a boy can wash a blackboard," a teacher was
heard to say, "I'll promote him."

I asked Mrs. R. how other Negroes felt about her
having had G. reassigned.

"Well, a lot of them don't like it," she said—though
I gathered that they did not say so to her. As school

time approached, more and more people asked her, "Are you going to send him?" "Well," she told them, "the man says the door is open and I feel like, yes, I'm going to go on and send him."

Out of a population of some fifty thousand Negroes, there had been only forty-five applications. People had said that they would send their children, had talked about it, had made plans; but, as the time drew near, when the application blanks were actually in their hands, they said, "I don't believe I'll sign this right now. I'll sign it later." Or, "I been thinking about this. I don't believe I'll send him right now."

"Why?" I asked. But to this she couldn't, or wouldn't, give me any answer.

I asked if there had been any reprisals taken against herself or her husband, if she was worried while G. was at school all day. She said that, no, there had been no reprisals, though some white people, under the pretext of giving her good advice, had expressed disapproval of her action. But she herself doesn't have a job and so doesn't risk losing one. Nor, she told me, had anyone said anything to her husband, who, however, by her own proud suggestion, is extremely closemouthed. And it developed later that he was not working at his regular trade but at something else.

As to whether she was worried, "No," she told me; in much the same way that G., when asked about the blockade, had said, "Nothing, sir." In her case it was easier to see what she meant: she hoped for the best and would not allow herself, in the meantime, to lose her head. "I don't feel like nothing's going to happen," she said, soberly. "I *hope* not. But I know if anybody tries to harm me or any one of my children, I'm going to strike back with all my strength. I'm going to strike them in God's name."

G., in the meantime, on the sofa with his books, was preparing himself for the next school day. His face was as impassive as ever and I found myself wondering—again—how he managed to face what must surely have been the worst moment of his day—the morning, when he opened his eyes and realized that it was all to be gone through again. Insults, and incipient violence, teachers, and—exams.

"One among so many," his mother said, "that's kind of rough."

"Do you think you'll make it?" I asked him. "Would you rather go back to ——— High?"

"No," he said, "I'll make it. I ain't going back."

"He ain't thinking about going back," said his mother —proudly and sadly. I began to suspect that the boy managed to support the extreme tension of his situation by means of a nearly fanatical concentration on his schoolwork; by holding in the center of his mind the issue on which, when the deal went down, others would be *forced* to judge him. Pride and silence were his weapons. Pride comes naturally, and soon, to a Negro, but even his mother, I felt, was worried about G.'s silence, though she was too wise to break it. For what was all this doing to him really?

"It's hard enough," the boy said later, still in control but with flashing eyes, "to keep quiet and keep walking when they call you nigger. But if anybody ever spits on me, I *know* I'll have to fight."

His mother laughs, laughs to ease them both, then looks at me and says, "I wonder sometimes what makes white folks so mean."

This is a recurring question among Negroes, even among the most "liberated"—which epithet is meant, of course, to describe the writer. The next day, with this question (more elegantly phrased) still beating in my mind, I visited the principal of G.'s new high school. But he didn't look "mean" and he wasn't "mean": he was a thin, young man of about my age, bewildered and in trouble. I asked him how things were working out, what he thought about it, what he thought would happen—in the long run, or the short.

"Well, I've got a job to do," he told me, "and I'm going to do it." He said that there hadn't been any trouble and that he didn't expect any. "Many students, after all, never see G. at all." None of the children have harmed him and the teachers are, apparently, carrying out their rather tall orders, which are to be kind to G. and, at the same time, to treat him like any other student.

I asked him to describe to me the incident, on the
second day of school, when G.'s entrance had been
blocked by the students. He told me that it was nothing
at all—"It was a gesture more than anything else." He
had simply walked out and spoken to the students and
brought G. inside. "I've seen them do the same thing to
other kids when they were kidding," he said. I imagine
that he would like to be able to place this incident in
the same cheerful if rowdy category, despite the shouts
(which he does not mention) of "nigger-lover!"

Which epithet does not, in any case, describe him at
all.

"Why," I asked, "is G. the only Negro student here?"
According to this city's pupil-assignment plan, a plan
designed to allow the least possible integration over the
longest possible period of time, G. was the only Negro
student who qualified.

"And, anyway," he said, "I don't think it's right for
colored children to come to white schools just *because*
they're white."

"Well," I began, "even if you don't like it . . ."

"Oh," he said quickly, raising his head and looking
at me sideways, "I never said I didn't like it."

And then he explained to me, with difficulty, that it
was simply contrary to everything he'd ever seen or believed. He'd never dreamed of a mingling of the races;
had never lived that way himself and didn't suppose that
he ever would; in the same way, he added, perhaps a

trifle defensively, that he only associated with a certain stratum of white people. But, "I've never seen a colored person toward whom I had any hatred or ill-will."

His eyes searched mine as he said this and I knew that he was wondering if I believed him.

I certainly did believe him; he impressed me as being a very gentle and honorable man. But I could not avoid wondering if he had ever really *looked* at a Negro and wondered about the life, the aspirations, the universal humanity hidden behind the dark skin. As I wondered, when he told me that race relations in his city were "excellent" and had not been strained by recent developments, how on earth he managed to hold on to this delusion.

I later got back to my interrupted question, which I phrased more tactfully.

"Even though it's very difficult for all concerned— this situation—doesn't it occur to you that the reason colored children wish to come to white schools isn't because they want to be with white people but simply because they want a better education?"

"Oh, I don't know," he replied, "it seems to me that colored schools are just as good as white schools." I wanted to ask him on what evidence he had arrived at this conclusion and also how they could possibly be "as good" in view of the kind of life they came out of, and perpetuated, and the dim prospects faced by all but

the most exceptional or ruthless Negro students. But I
only suggested that G. and his family, who certainly
should have known, so thoroughly disagreed with him
that they had been willing to risk G.'s present well-
being and his future psychological and mental health in
order to bring about a change in his environment. Nor
did I mention the lack of enthusiasm evinced by G.'s
mother when musing on the prospect of a fair grand-
child. There seemed no point in making this man any
more a victim of his heritage than he so gallantly was
already.

"Still," I said at last, after a rather painful pause,
"I should think that the trouble in this situation is that
it's very hard for *you* to face a child and treat him un-
justly because of something for which he is no more
responsible than—than *you* are."

The eyes came to life then, or a veil fell, and I found
myself staring at a man in anguish. The eyes were full
of pain and bewilderment and he nodded his head.
This was the impossibility which he faced every day.
And I imagined that his tribe would increase, in sudden leaps and bounds was already increasing.

For segregation has worked brilliantly in the South,
and, in fact, in the nation, to this extent: it has allowed
white people, with scarcely any pangs of conscience
whatever, to *create*, in every generation, only the Negro
they wished to see. As the walls come down they will be
forced to take another, harder look at the shiftless and

the menial and will be forced into a wonder concerning them which cannot fail to be agonizing. It is not an easy thing to be forced to re-examine a way of life and to speculate, in a personal way, on the general injustice.

"What do you think," I asked him, "will happen? What do you think the future holds?"

He gave a strained laugh and said he didn't know. "I don't want to think about it." Then, "I'm a religious man," he said, "and I believe the Creator will always help us find a way to solve our problems. If a man loses that, he's lost everything he had." I agreed, struck by the look in his eyes.

"You're from the North?" he asked me, abruptly.

"Yes," I said.

"Well," he said, "you've got your troubles too."

"Ah, yes, we certainly do," I admitted, and shook hands and left him. I did not say what I was thinking, that our troubles were the same trouble and that, unless we were very swift and honest, what is happening in the South today will be happening in the North tomorrow.

6. Nobody Knows My Name:

A Letter from the South

I walked down the street, didn't
have on no hat,
Asking everybody I meet,
Where's my man at?
—Ma Rainey

Negroes in the north are right when they refer to the South as the Old Country. A Negro born in the North who finds himself in the South is in a position similar to that of the son of the Italian emigrant who finds himself in Italy, near the village where his father first saw the light of day. Both are in countries they have never seen, but which they cannot fail to recognize. The landscape has always been familiar; the speech is archaic, but it rings a bell; and so do the ways of the people, though their ways are not his ways. Everywhere he turns, the revenant finds himself reflected. He sees himself as he was before he was born, perhaps; or as the man he would have become, had he actually been born in this place. He sees the world, from an angle odd indeed, in which his fathers awaited his arrival, perhaps in the very house in which he narrowly avoided being born. He sees, in effect, his ancestors, who, in everything they do and are, proclaim his inescapable identity. And the Northern Negro in the South sees, whatever he or anyone else may wish to believe, that his ancestors are both white and black. The white men, flesh of his flesh, hate him for that very reason. On the other hand, there is scarcely any way for him to join the black community in the South: for both he and this community are in the grip of the immense illusion that their state is more miserable than his own.

This illusion owes everything to the great American illusion that our state is a state to be envied by other people: we are powerful, and we are rich. But our power makes us uncomfortable and we handle it very ineptly. The principal effect of our material well-being has been to set the children's teeth on edge. If we ourselves were not so fond of this illusion, we might understand ourselves and other peoples better than we do, and be enabled to help them understand us. I am very often tempted to believe that this illusion is all that is left of the great dream that was to have become America; whether this is so or not, this illusion certainly prevents us from making America what we say we want it to be.

But let us put aside, for the moment, these subversive speculations. In the fall of last year, my plane hovered over the rust-red earth of Georgia. I was past thirty, and I had never seen this land before. I pressed my face against the window, watching the earth come closer;

soon we were just above the tops of trees. I could not suppress the thought that this earth had acquired its color from the blood that had dripped down from these trees. My mind was filled with the image of a black man, younger than I, perhaps, or my own age, hanging from a tree, while white men watched him and cut his sex from him with a knife.

My father must have seen such sights—he was very old when he died—or heard of them, or had this danger touch him. The Negro poet I talked to in Washington, much younger than my father, perhaps twenty years older than myself, remembered such things very vividly, had a long tale to tell, and counseled me to think back on those days as a means of steadying the soul. I was to remember that time, whatever else it had failed to do, nevertheless had passed, that the situation, whether or not it was better, was certainly no longer the same. I was to remember that Southern Negroes had endured things I could not imagine; but this did not really place me at such a great disadvantage, since they clearly had been unable to imagine what awaited them in Harlem. I remembered the Scottsboro case, which I had followed as a child. I remembered Angelo Herndon and wondered, again, whatever had become of him. I remembered the soldier in uniform blinded by an enraged white man, just after the Second World War. There had been many such incidents after the First War, which was one of the reasons I had been born in Harlem. I remembered Willie

McGhee, Emmett Till, and the others. My younger brothers had visited Atlanta some years before. I remembered
what they had told me about it. One of my brothers, in
uniform, had had his front teeth kicked out by a white
officer. I remembered my mother telling us how she had
wept and prayed and tried to kiss the venom out of her
suicidally embittered son. (She managed to do it, too;
heaven only knows what she herself was feeling, whose
father and brothers had lived and died down here.) I
remembered myself as a very small boy, already so
bitter about the pledge of allegiance that I could
scarcely bring myself to say it, and never, never believed it.

I was, in short, but one generation removed from the
South, which was now undergoing a new convulsion over
whether black children had the same rights, or capaci-
ties, for education as did the children of white people.
This is a criminally frivolous dispute, absolutely un-
worthy of this nation; and it is being carried on, in
complete bad faith, by completely uneducated people.
(We do not trust educated people and rarely, alas, produce them, for we do not trust the independence of mind
which alone makes a genuine education possible.) Educated people, of any color, are so extremely rare that it
is unquestionably one of the first tasks of a nation to
open all of its schools to all of its citizens. But the dispute has actually nothing to do with education, as some
among the eminently uneducated know. It has to do with

political power and it has to do with sex. And this is a
nation which, most unluckily, knows very little about
either.

The city of Atlanta, according to my notes, is "big,
wholly segregated, sprawling; population variously
given as six hundred thousand or one million, depend-
ing on whether one goes beyond or remains within the
city limits. Negroes 25 to 30 per cent of the population.
Racial relations, on the record, can be described as fair,
considering that this is the state of Georgia. Growing in-
dustrial town. Racial relations manipulated by the mayor
and a fairly strong Negro middle class. This works
mainly in the areas of compromise and concession and
has very little effect on the bulk of the Negro population
and none whatever on the rest of the state. No integration, pending or actual." Also, it seemed to me that the
Negroes in Atlanta were "very vividly *city* Negroes"—
they seemed less patient than their rural brethren, more
dangerous, or at least more unpredictable. And: "Have
seen one wealthy Negro section, very pretty, but with an
unpaved road. . . . The section in which I am living is
composed of frame houses in various stages of disrepair
and neglect, in which two and three families live, often
sharing a single toilet. This is the other side of the
tracks; literally, I mean. It is located, as I am told is the
case in many Southern cities, just beyond the under-
pass." Atlanta contains a high proportion of Negroes
who own their own homes and exist, visibly anyway, in-

dependently of the white world. Southern towns distrust
this class and do everything in their power to prevent its
appearance. But it is a class which has a certain useful-
ness in Southern cities. There is an incipient war, in
fact, between Southern cities and Southern towns—between the city, that is, and the state—which we will discuss later. Little Rock is an ominous example of this and
it is likely—indeed, it is certain—that we will see many
more such examples before the present crisis is over.

Before arriving in Atlanta I had spent several days in
Charlotte, North Carolina. This is a bourgeois town,
Presbyterian, pretty—if you like towns—and socially
so hermetic that it contains scarcely a single decent
restaurant. I was told that Negroes there are not even
licensed to become electricians or plumbers. I was also
told, several times, by white people, that "race relations"
there were excellent. I failed to find a single Negro who
agreed with this, which is the usual story of "race relations" in this country. Charlotte, a town of 165,000, was
in a ferment when I was there because, of its 50,000
Negroes, four had been assigned to previously all-white
schools, one to each school. In fact, by the time I got
there, there were only three. Dorothy Counts, the daughter of a Presbyterian minister, after several days of
being stoned and spat on by the mob—"spit," a woman
told me, "was hanging from the hem of Dorothy's dress"
—had withdrawn from Harding High. Several white students, I was told, had called—not called *on*—Miss

Counts, to beg her to stick it out. Harry Golden, editor
of *The Carolina Israelite*, suggested that the "hoodlum
element" might not so have shamed the town and the
nation if several of the town's leading businessmen had
personally escorted Miss Counts to school.

I saw the Negro schools in Charlotte, saw, on street
corners, several of their alumnae, and read about others
who had been sentenced to the chain gang. This solved
the mystery of just what made Negro parents send their
children out to face mobs. White people do not understand this because they do not know, and do not want to
know, that the alternative to this ordeal is nothing less
than a lifelong ordeal. Those Negro parents who spend
their days trembling for their children and the rest of
their time praying that their children have not been too
badly damaged inside, are not doing this out of "ideals"
or "convictions" or because they are in the grip of a
perverse desire to send their children where "they are
not wanted." They are doing it because they want the
child to receive the education which will allow him to
defeat, possibly escape, and not impossibly help one day
abolish the stifling environment in which they see, daily,
so many children perish.

This is certainly not the purpose, still less the effect,
of most Negro schools. It is hard enough, God knows,
under the best of circumstances, to get an education in
this country. White children are graduated yearly who
can neither read, write, nor think, and who are in a state

of the most abysmal ignorance concerning the world around them. But at least they are white. They are under the illusion—which, since they are so badly educated, sometimes has a fatal tenacity—that they can do whatever they want to do. Perhaps that is exactly what they *are* doing, in which case we had best all go down in prayer.

The level of Negro education, obviously, is even lower than the general level. The general level is low because, as I have said, Americans have so little respect for genuine intellectual effort. The Negro level is low because the education of Negroes occurs in, and is designed to perpetuate, a segregated society. This, in the first place, and no matter how much money the South boasts of spending on Negro schools, is utterly demoralizing. It creates a situation in which the Negro teacher is soon as powerless as his students. (There are exceptions among the teachers as there are among the students, but, in this country surely, schools have not been built for the exceptional. And, though white people often seem to expect Negroes to produce nothing but exceptions, the fact is that Negroes are really just like everybody else. Some of them are exceptional and most of them are not.)

The teachers are answerable to the Negro principal, whose power over the teachers is absolute but whose power with the school board is slight. As for this principal, he has arrived at the summit of his career; rarely indeed can he go any higher. He has his pension to look forward to, and he consoles himself, meanwhile, with his status among the "better class of Negroes." This class includes few, if any, of his students and by no means all of his teachers. The teachers, as long as they remain in this school system, and they certainly do not have much choice, can only aspire to become the principal one day. Since not all of them will make it, a great deal of the energy which ought to go into their vocation goes into the usual bitter, purposeless rivalry. They are underpaid and ill treated by the white world and rubbed raw by it every day; and it is altogether understandable that they, very shortly, cannot bear the sight of their students. The children know this; it is hard to fool young people. They also know why they are going to an overcrowded, outmoded plant, in classes so large that even the most strictly attentive student, the most gifted teacher cannot but feel himself slowly drowning in the sea of general helplessness.

It is not to be wondered at, therefore, that the violent distractions of puberty, occurring in such a cage, annually take their toll, sending female children into the maternity wards and male children into the streets. It is not to be wondered at that a boy, one day, decides that if all this studying is going to prepare him only to be a porter or an elevator boy—or his teacher—well, then, the hell with it. And there they go, with an overwhelming bitterness which they will dissemble all their lives,

an unceasing effort which completes their ruin. They be-
come the menial or the criminal or the shiftless, the
Negroes whom segregation has produced and whom the
South uses to prove that segregation is right.

In Charlotte, too, I received some notion of what the
South means by "time to adjust." The NAACP there had
been trying for six years before Black Monday to make
the city fathers honor the "separate but equal" statute
and do something about the situation in Negro schools.
Nothing whatever was done. After Black Monday, Charlotte begged for "time": and what she did with this time
was work out legal stratagems designed to get the least
possible integration over the longest possible period. In
August of 1955, Governor Hodges, a moderate, went on
the air with the suggestion that Negroes segregate themselves voluntarily—for the good, as he put it, of both
races. Negroes seeming to be unmoved by this moderate
proposal, the Klan reappeared in the counties and was
still active there when I left. So, no doubt, are the boys
on the chain gang.

But "Charlotte," I was told, "is not the South." I was
told, "You haven't seen the South yet." Charlotte seemed
quite Southern enough for me, but, in fact, the people in
Charlotte were right. One of the reasons for this is that
the South is not the monolithic structure which, from the
North, it appears to be, but a most various and divided
region. It clings to the myth of its past but it is being
inexorably changed, meanwhile, by an entirely un-

mythical present: its habits and its self-interest are at war. Everyone in the South feels this and this is why there is such panic on the bottom and such impotence on the top.

It must also be said that the racial setup in the South is not, for a Negro, very different from the racial setup in the North. It is the etiquette which is baffling, not the spirit. Segregation is unofficial in the North and official in the South, a crucial difference that does nothing, nevertheless, to alleviate the lot of most Northern Negroes. But we will return to this question when we discuss the relationship between the Southern cities and states.

Atlanta, however, *is* the South. It is the South in this respect, that it has a very bitter interracial history. This is written in the faces of the people and one feels it in the air. It was on the outskirts of Atlanta that I first felt how the Southern landscape—the trees, the silence, the liquid heat, and the fact that one always seems to be traveling great distances—seems designed for violence, seems, almost, to demand it. What passions cannot be unleashed on a dark road in a Southern night! Everything seems so sensual, so languid, and so private. Desire can be acted out here; over this fence, behind that tree, in the darkness, there; and no one will see, no one will ever know. Only the night is watching and the night was made for desire. Protestantism is the wrong religion for people in such climates; America is perhaps the last nation in which such a climate belongs. In the Southern night everything seems possible, the most private, unspeakable longings; but then arrives the Southern day, as hard and brazen as the night was soft and dark. It brings what was done in the dark to light. It must have seemed something like this for those people who made the region what it is today. It must have caused them great pain. Perhaps the master who had coupled with his slave saw his guilt in his wife's pale eyes in the morning. And the wife saw his children in the slave quarters, saw the way his concubine, the sensual-looking black girl, looked at her—a woman, after all, and scarcely less sensual, but white. The youth, nursed and raised by the black Mammy whose arms had then held all that there was of warmth and love and desire, and still confounded by the dreadful taboos set up between himself and her progeny, must have wondered, after his first experiment with black flesh, where, under the blazing heavens, he could hide. And the white man must have seen his guilt written somewhere else, seen it all the time, even if his sin was merely lust, even if his sin lay in nothing but his power: in the eyes of the black man. He may not have stolen his woman, but he had certainly stolen his freedom—this black man, who had a body like his, and passions like his, and a ruder, more erotic beauty. How many times has the Southern day come up to find that black man, sexless, hanging from a tree!

It was an old black man in Atlanta who looked into

my eyes and directed me into my first segregated bus. I
have spent a long time thinking about that man. I never
saw him again. I cannot describe the look which passed
between us, as I asked him for directions, but it made
me think, at once, of Shakespeare's "the oldest have
borne most." It made me think of the blues: *Now, when
a woman gets the blues, Lord, she hangs her head and
cries. But when a man gets the blues, Lord, he grabs a
train and rides.* It was borne in on me, suddenly, just
why these men had so often been grabbing freight trains
as the evening sun went down. And it was, perhaps, because I was getting on a segregated bus, and wondering
how Negroes had borne this and other indignities for
so long, that this man so struck me. He seemed to know
what I was feeling. His eyes seemed to say that what I
was feeling he had been feeling, at much higher pressure, all his life. But my eyes would never see the hell
his eyes had seen. And this hell was, simply, that he had
never in his life owned anything, not his wife, not his
house, not his child, which could not, at any instant, be
taken from him by the power of white people. This is
what paternalism means. And for the rest of the time
that I was in the South I watched the eyes of old black
men.

Atlanta's well-to-do Negroes never takes buses, for
they all have cars. The section in which they live is
quite far away from the poor Negro section. They own,

or at least are paying for, their own homes. They drive to work and back, and have cocktails and dinner with each other. They see very little of the white world; but they are cut off from the black world, too.

Now, of course, this last statement is not literally true. The teachers teach Negroes, the lawyers defend them. The ministers preach to them and bury them, and others insure their lives, pull their teeth, and cure their ailments. Some of the lawyers work with the NAACP and help push test cases through the courts. (If anything, by the way, disproves the charge of "extremism" which has so often been made against this organization, it is the fantastic care and patience such legal efforts demand.) Many of the teachers work very hard to bolster the morale of their students and prepare them for their new responsibilities; nor did those I met fool themselves about the *hideous* system under which they work. So when I say that they are cut off from the black world, I am not sneering, which, indeed, I scarcely have any right to do. I am talking about their position as a class —*if* they are a class—and their role in a very complex and shaky social structure.

The wealthier Negroes are, at the moment, very useful for the administration of the city of Atlanta, for they represent there the potential, at least, of interracial communication. That this phrase is a euphemism, in Atlanta as elsewhere, becomes clear when one considers how astonishingly little has been communicated in all these

generations. What the phrase almost always has reference to is the fact that, in a given time and place, the
Negro vote is of sufficient value to force politicians to
bargain for it. What interracial communication also
refers to is that Atlanta is really growing and thriving,
and because it wants to make even more money, it would
like to prevent incidents that disturb the peace, discour-
age investments, and permit test cases, which the city of
Atlanta would certainly lose, to come to the courts. Once
this happens, as it certainly will one day, the state of
Georgia will be up in arms and the present administration of the city will be out of power. I did not meet a
soul in Atlanta (I naturally did not meet any members
of the White Citizen's Council, not, anyway, to talk to)
who did not pray that the present mayor would be re-
elected. Not that they loved him particularly, but it is
his administration which holds off the holocaust.

Now this places Atlanta's wealthy Negroes in a really
quite sinister position. Though both they and the mayor
are devoted to keeping the peace, their aims and his are
not, and cannot be, the same. Many of those lawyers are
working day and night on test cases which the mayor is
doing his best to keep out of court. The teachers spend
their working day attempting to destroy in their students
—and it is not too much to say, in themselves—those
habits of inferiority which form one of the principal
cornerstones of segregation as it is practiced in the
South. Many of the parents listen to speeches by people
like Senator Russell and find themselves unable to sleep

at night. They are in the extraordinary position of being
compelled to work for the destruction of all they have
bought so dearly—their homes, their comfort, the safety
of their children. But the safety of their children is
merely comparative; it is all that their comparative
strength as a class has bought them so far; and they
are not safe, really, as long as the bulk of Atlanta's
Negroes live in such darkness. On any night, in that
other part of town, a policeman may beat up one Negro
too many, or some Negro or some white man may simply
go berserk. This is all it takes to drive so delicately bal-
anced a city mad. And the island on which these Negroes
have built their handsome houses will simply disappear.

This is not at all in the interests of Atlanta, and almost
everyone there knows it. Left to itself, the city might
grudgingly work out compromises designed to reduce
the tension and raise the level of Negro life. But it is not
left to itself; it belongs to the state of Georgia. The
Negro vote has no power in the state, and the governor
of Georgia—that "third-rate man," Atlantans call him—
makes great political capital out of keeping the Negroes
in their place. When six Negro ministers attempted to
create a test case by ignoring the segregation ordinance
on the buses, the governor was ready to declare martial
law and hold the ministers incommunicado. It was the
mayor who prevented this, who somehow squashed all
publicity, treated the ministers with every outward sign
of respect, and it is his office which is preventing the case
from coming into court. And remember that it was the

governor of Arkansas, in an insane bid for political power, who created the present crisis in Little Rock—against the will of most of its citizens and against the will of the mayor.

This war between the Southern cities and states is of the utmost importance, not only for the South, but for the nation. The Southern states are still very largely governed by people whose political lives, insofar, at least, as they are able to conceive of life or politics, are dependent on the people in the rural regions. It might, indeed, be more honorable to try to guide these people out of their pain and ignorance instead of locking them within it, and battening on it; but it is, admittedly, a difficult task to try to tell people the truth and it is clear that most Southern politicians have no intention of attempting it. The attitude of these people can only have the effect of stiffening the already implacable Negro resistance, and this attitude is absolutely certain, sooner or later, to create great trouble in the cities. When a race riot occurs in Atlanta, it will not spread merely to Birmingham, for example. (Birmingham is a doomed city.) The trouble will spread to every metropolitan center in the nation which has a significant Negro population. And this is not only because the ties between Northern and Southern Negroes are still very close. It is because the nation, the entire nation, has spent a hundred years avoiding the question of the place of the black man in it.

That this has done terrible things to black men is not

even a question. "Integration," said a very light Negro
to me in Alabama, "has always worked very well in the
South, after the sun goes down." "It's not miscegenation," said another Negro to me, "unless a black man's
involved." Now, I talked to many Southern liberals who
were doing their best to bring integration about in the
South, but met scarcely a single Southerner who did not
weep for the passing of the old order. They were perfectly sincere, too, and, within their limits, they were
right. They pointed out how Negroes and whites in the
South had loved each other, they recounted to me tales
of devotion and heroism which the old order had produced, and which, now, would never come again. But
the old black men I looked at down there—those same
black men that the Southern liberal had loved; for whom,
until now, the Southern liberal—and not only the liberal
—has been willing to undergo great inconvenience and
danger—they were not weeping. Men do not like to be
protected, it emasculates them. This is what black men
know, it is the reality they have lived with; it is what
white men do not want to know. It is not a pretty thing to
be a father and be ultimately dependent on the power
and kindness of some other man for the well-being of
your house.

But what this evasion of the Negro's humanity has
done to the nation is not so well known. The really striking thing, for me, in the South was this dreadful paradox,
that the black men were stronger than the white. I do not

know how they did it, but it certainly has something to do with that as yet unwritten history of the Negro woman. What it comes to, finally, is that the nation has spent a large part of its time and energy looking away from one of the principal facts of its life. This failure to look reality in the face diminishes a nation as it diminishes a person, and it can only be described as unmanly. And in exactly the same way that the South imagines that it "knows" the Negro, the North imagines that it has set him free. Both camps are deluded. Human freedom is a complex, difficult—and private—thing. If we can liken life, for a moment, to a furnace, then freedom is the fire which burns away illusion. Any honest examination of the national life proves how far we are from the standard of human freedom with which we began. The recovery of this standard demands of everyone who loves this country a hard look at himself, for the greatest achievements must begin somewhere, and they always begin with the person. If we are not capable of this examination, we may yet become one of the most distinguished and monumental failures in the history of nations.

7. Faulkner and Desegregation

ANY REAL CHANGE IMPLIES THE breakup of the world as one has always known it, the loss of all that gave one an identity, the end of safety. And at such a moment, unable to see and not daring to imagine what the future will now bring forth, one clings to what one knew, or thought one knew; to what one possessed or dreamed that one possessed. Yet, it is only when a man is able, without bitterness or self-pity, to surrender a dream he has long cherished or a privilege he has long possessed that he is set free—he has set himself free—for higher dreams, for greater privileges. All men have gone through this, go through it, each according to his degree, throughout their lives. It is one of the irreducible facts of life. And remembering this, especially since I am a Negro, affords me almost my only means of understanding what is happening in the minds and hearts of white Southerners today.

For the arguments with which the bulk of relatively articulate white Southerners of good will have met the necessity of desegregation have no value whatever as arguments, being almost entirely and helplessly dishonest, when not, indeed, insane. After more than two hundred years in slavery and ninety years of quasi-freedom, it is hard to think very highly of William Faulkner's advice to "go slow." "They don't mean go slow," Thurgood Marshall is reported to have said, "they mean don't go." Nor is the squire of Oxford very persuasive when he suggests that white Southerners, left to their own devices, will realize that their own social structure looks silly to the rest of the world and correct it of their own accord. It has looked silly, to use Faulkner's rather strange adjective, for a long time; so far from trying to correct it, Southerners, who seem to be characterized by a species of defiance most perverse when it is most despairing, have clung to it, at incalculable cost to themselves, as the only conceivable and as an absolutely sacrosanct way of life. They have never seriously conceded that their social structure was mad. They have insisted, on the contrary, that everyone who criticized it was mad.

Faulkner goes further. He concedes the madness and moral wrongness of the South but at the same time he raises it to the level of a mystique which makes it somehow unjust to discuss Southern society in the same terms in which one would discuss any other society. "Our position is wrong and untenable," says Faulkner, "but it is not wise to keep an emotional people off balance." This if it means anything, can only mean that this "emotional people" have been swept "off balance" by the pressure of recent events, that is, the Supreme Court decision outlawing segregation. When the pressure is taken off—and not an instant before—this "emotional people" will presumably find themselves once again on balance and will then be able to free themselves of an "obsolescence in [their] own land" in their own way and, of course, in their own time. The question left begging is what, in their history to date, affords any evidence that they have any desire or capacity to do this. And it is, I suppose, impertinent to ask just what Negroes are supposed to do while the South works out what, in Faulkner's rhetoric, becomes something very closely resembling a high and noble tragedy.

The sad truth is that whatever modifications have been effected in the social structure of the South since the Reconstruction, and any alleviations of the Negro's lot within it, are due to great and incessant pressure, very little of it indeed from within the South. That the North has been guilty of Pharisaism in its dealing with the South does not negate the fact that much of this pressure has come from the North. That some—not nearly as many as Faulkner would like to believe—Southern Negroes prefer, or are afraid of changing, the status quo does not negate the fact that it is the Southern Negro himself who, year upon year, and generation upon generation, has kept the Southern waters troubled. As far as the Negro's life in the South is concerned, the NAACP is the only organization which has struggled, with admirable single-mindedness and skill, to raise him to the level of a citizen. For this reason alone, and quite apart from the individual heroism of many of its Southern members, it cannot be equated, as Faulkner equates it, with the pathological Citizen's Council. One organization is working within the law and the other is working against and outside it. Faulkner's threat to leave the "middle of the road" where he has, presumably, all these years, been working for the benefit of Negroes, reduces itself to a more or less up-to-date version of the Southern threat to secede from the Union.

Faulkner—among so many others!—is so plaintive concerning this "middle of the road" from which "extremist" elements of both races are driving him that it does not seem unfair to ask just what he has been doing there until now. Where is the evidence of the struggle he has been carrying on there on behalf of the Negro? Why, if he and his enlightened confreres in the South have been boring from within to destroy segregation, do they react with such panic when the walls show any signs of falling? Why—and how—does one move from the middle of the road where one was aiding Negroes into the streets—to shoot them?

Now it is easy enough to state flatly that Faulkner's

middle of the road does not—cannot—exist and that he
is guilty of great emotional and intellectual dishonesty
in pretending that it does. I think this is why he clings to
his fantasy. It is easy enough to accuse him of hypocrisy
when he speaks of man being "indestructible because
of his simple will to freedom." But he is not being hypocritical; he means it. It is only that Man is one thing
—a rather unlucky abstraction in this case—and the
Negroes he has always known, so fatally tied up in his
mind with his grandfather's slaves, are quite another.
He is at his best, and is perfectly sincere, when he de-
clares, in *Harpers*, "To live anywhere in the world today
and be against equality because of race or color is like
living in Alaska and being against snow. We have already got snow. And as with the Alaskan, merely to live
in armistice with it is not enough. Like the Alaskan, we
had better use it." And though this seems to be flatly
opposed to his statement (in an interview printed in *The
Reporter*) that, if it came to a contest between the federal government and Mississippi, he would fight for
Mississippi, "even if it meant going out into the streets
and shooting Negroes," he means that, too. Faulkner
means everything he says, means them all at once, and
with very nearly the same intensity. This is why his
statements demand our attention. He has perhaps never
before more concretely expressed what it means to be a
Southerner.

What seems to define the Southerner, in his own mind

at any rate, is his relationship to the North, that is to the rest of the Republic, a relationship which can at the very best be described as uneasy. It is apparently very difficult to be at once a Southerner and an American; so difficult that many of the South's most independent minds are forced into the American exile; which is not, of course, without its aggravating, circular effect on the interior and public life of the South. A Bostonian, say, who leaves Boston is not regarded by the citizenry he has abandoned with the same venomous distrust as is the Southerner who leaves the South. The citizenry of Boston do not consider that they have been abandoned, much less betrayed. It is only the American Southerner who seems to be fighting, in his own entrails, a peculiar, ghastly, and perpetual war with all the rest of the country. ("Didn't you say," demanded a Southern woman of Robert Penn Warren, "that you was born down here, used to live right near here?" And when he agreed that this was so: "Yes . . . but you never said where you living now!")

The difficulty, perhaps, is that the Southerner clings to two entirely antithetical doctrines, two legends, two histories. Like all other Americans, he must subscribe, and is to some extent controlled by the beliefs and the principles expressed in the Constitution; at the same time, these beliefs and principles seem determined to destroy the South. He is, on the one hand, the proud citizen of a free society and, on the other, is committed to a society

which has not yet dared to free itself of the necessity of
naked and brutal oppression. He is part of a country
which boasts that it has never lost a war; but he is also
the representative of a conquered nation. I have not seen
a single statement of Faulkner's concerning desegregation which does not inform us that his family has lived
in the same part of Mississippi for generations, that his
great-grandfather owned slaves, and that his ancestors
fought and died in the Civil War. And so compelling is
the image of ruin, gallantry and death thus evoked that
it demands a positive effort of the imagination to remember that slaveholding Southerners were not the only
people who perished in that war. Negroes and Northerners were also blown to bits. American history, as opposed to Southern history, proves that Southerners were
not the only slaveholders, Negroes were not even the
only slaves. And the segregation which Faulkner sancti-
fies by references to Shiloh, Chickamauga, and Gettys-
burg does not extend back that far, is in fact scarcely
as old as the century. The "racial condition" which
Faulkner will not have changed by "mere force of law
or economic threat" was imposed by precisely these
means. The Southern tradition, which is, after all, all
that Faulkner is talking about, is not a tradition at all:
when Faulkner evokes it, he is simply evoking a legend
which contains an accusation. And that accusation,
stated far more simply than it should be, is that the
North, in winning the war, left the South only one means

of asserting its identity and that means was the Negro.

"My people owned slaves," says Faulkner, "and the very obligation we have to take care of these people is morally bad." "This problem is . . . far beyond the moral one it is and still was a hundred years ago, in 1860, when many Southerners, including Robert Lee, recognized it as a moral one at the very instant they in turn elected to champion the underdog because that underdog was blood and kin and home." But the North escaped scot-free. For one thing, in freeing the slave, it established a moral superiority over the South which the South has not learned to live with until today; and this despite—or possibly because of—the fact that this moral superiority was bought, after all, rather cheaply. The North was no better prepared than the South, as it turned out, to make citizens of former slaves, but it was able, as the South was not, to wash its hands of the matter. Men who knew that slavery was wrong were forced, nevertheless, to fight to perpetuate it because they were unable to turn against "blood and kin and home." And when blood and kin and home were defeated, they found themselves, more than ever, committed: committed, in effect, to a way of life which was as unjust and crippling as it was inescapable. In sum, the North, by freeing the slaves of their masters, robbed the masters of any possibility of freeing themselves of the slaves.

When Faulkner speaks, then, of the "middle of the

road," he is simply speaking of the hope—which was always unrealistic and is now all but smashed—that the white Southerner, with no coercion from the rest of the nation, will lift himself above his ancient, crippling bitterness and refuse to add to his already intolerable burden of blood-guiltiness. But this hope would seem to be absolutely dependent on a social and psychological stasis which simply does not exist. "Things have been getting better," Faulkner tells us, "for a long time. Only six Negroes were killed by whites in Mississippi last year, according to police figures." Faulkner surely knows how little consolation this offers a Negro and he also knows something about "police figures" in the Deep South. And he knows, too, that murder is not the worst thing that can happen to a man, black or white. But murder may be the worst thing a man can do. Faulkner is not trying to save Negroes, who are, in his view, already saved; who, having refused to be destroyed by terror, are far stronger than the terrified white populace; and who have, moreover, fatally, from his point of view, the weight of the federal government behind them. He is trying to save "whatever good remains in those white people." The time he pleads for is the time in which the Southerner will come to terms with himself, will cease fleeing from his conscience, and achieve, in the words of Robert Penn Warren, "moral identity." And he surely believes, with Warren, that "Then in a country where moral identity is hard to come by, the

South, because it has had to deal concretely with a moral problem, may offer some leadership. And we need any we can get. If we are to break out of the national rhythm, the rhythm between complacency and panic."

But the time Faulkner asks for does not exist—and he is not the only Southerner who knows it. There is never time in the future in which we will work out our salvation. The challenge is in the moment, the time is always now.

8. In Search of a Majority:

An Address

I AM SUPPOSED TO SPEAK THIS evening on the goals of American society as they involve minority rights, but what I am really going to do is to invite you to join me in a series of speculations. Some of them are dangerous, some of them painful, all of them are reckless. It seems to me that before we can begin to speak of minority rights in this country, we've got to make some attempt to isolate or to define the majority.

Presumably the society in which we live is an expression—in some way—of the majority will. But it is not so easy to locate this majority. The moment one attempts to define this majority one is faced with several conundrums. Majority is not an expression of numbers, of numerical strength, for example. You may far outnumber your opposition and not be able to impose your will on them or even to modify the rigor with which they

impose their will on you, i.e., the Negroes in South
Africa or in some counties, some sections, of the American South. You may have beneath your hand all the
apparatus of power, political, military, state, and still
be unable to use these things to achieve your ends, which
is the problem faced by de Gaulle in Algeria and the
problem which faced Eisenhower when, largely because
of his own inaction, he was forced to send paratroopers
into Little Rock. Again, the most trenchant observers of
the scene in the South, those who are embattled there, feel
that the Southern mobs are not an expression of the
Southern majority will. Their impression is that these
mobs fill, so to speak, a moral vacuum and that the
people who form these mobs would be very happy to be
released from their pain, and their ignorance, if someone arrived to show them the way. I would be inclined to
agree with this, simply from what we know of human
nature. It is not my impression that people wish to become worse; they really wish to become better but very
often do not know how. Most people assume the position,
in a way, of the Jews in Egypt, who really wished to get
to the Promised Land but were afraid of the rigors of
the journey; and, of course, before you embark on a
journey the terrors of whatever may overtake you on
that journey live in the imagination and paralyze you.
It was through Moses, according to legend, that they
discovered, by undertaking this journey, how much they
could endure.

These speculations have led me a little bit ahead of myself. I suppose it can be said that there was a time in this country when an entity existed which could be called the majority, let's say a class, for the lack of a better word, which created the standards by which the country lived or which created the standards to which the country aspired. I am referring or have in mind, perhaps somewhat arbitrarily, the aristocracies of Virginia and New England. These were mainly of Anglo-Saxon stock and they created what Henry James was to refer to, not very much later, as our Anglo-American heritage, or Anglo-American connections. Now at no time did these men ever form anything resembling a popular majority. Their importance was that they kept alive and they bore witness to two elements of a man's life which are not greatly respected among us now: (1) the social forms, called manners, which prevent us from rubbing too abrasively against one another and (2) the interior life, or the life of the mind. These things were important; these things were realities for them and no matter how rough-hewn or dark the country was then, it is important to remember that this was also the time when people sat up in log cabins studying very hard by lamplight or candlelight. That they were better educated than we are now can be proved by comparing the political speeches of that time with those of our own day.

Now, what I have been trying to suggest in all this is

that the only useful definition of the word "majority" does not refer to numbers, and it does not refer to power. It refers to influence. Someone said, and said it very accurately, that what is honored in a country is cultivated there. If we apply this touchstone to American life we can scarcely fail to arrive at a very grim view of it. But I think we have to look grim facts in the face because if we don't, we can never hope to change them.

These vanished aristocracies, these vanished standard bearers, had several limitations, and not the least of these limitations was the fact that their standards were essentially nostalgic. They referred to a past condition; they referred to the achievements, the laborious achievements, of a stratified society; and what was evolving in America had nothing to do with the past. So inevitably what happened, putting it far too simply, was that the old forms gave way before the European tidal wave, gave way before the rush of Italians, Greeks, Spaniards, Irishmen, Poles, Persians, Norwegians, Swedes, Danes, wandering Jews from every nation under heaven, Turks, Armenians, Lithuanians, Japanese, Chinese, and Indians. Everybody was here suddenly in the melting pot, as we like to say, but without any intention of being melted. They were here because they had wanted to leave wherever they had been and they were here to make their lives, and achieve their futures, and to establish a new identity. I doubt if history has ever seen such a spectacle, such a conglomeration of hopes, fears, and de-

sires. I suggest, also, that they presented a problem for
the Puritan God, who had never heard of them and of
whom they had never heard. Almost always as they arrived, they took their places as a minority, a minority because their influence was so slight and because it was
their necessity to make themselves over in the image of
their new and unformed country. There were no longer
any universally accepted forms or standards, and since
all the roads to the achievement of an identity had vanished, the problem of status in American life became and
it remains today acute. In a way, status became a kind of
substitute for identity, and because money and the
things money can buy is the universally accepted symbol
here of status, we are often condemned as materialists.
In fact, we are much closer to being metaphysical because nobody has ever expected from things the mir-
acles that we expect.

Now I think it will be taken for granted that the Irish,
the Swedes, the Danes, etc., who came here can no
longer be considered in any serious way as minorities;
and the question of anti-Semitism presents too many
special features to be profitably discussed here tonight.
The American minorities can be placed on a kind of
color wheel. For example, when we think of the American boy, we don't usually think of a Spanish, Turkish, a
Greek, or a Mexican type, still less of an Oriental type.
We usually think of someone who is kind of a cross between the Teuton and the Celt, and I think it is interest-

ing to consider what this image suggests. Outrageous as
this image is, in most cases, it is the national self-image.
It is an image which suggests hard work and good clean
fun and chastity and piety and success. It leaves out of
account, of course, most of the people in the country,
and most of the facts of life, and there is not much point
in discussing those virtues it suggests, which are mainly
honored in the breach. The point is that it has almost
nothing to do with what or who an American really is.
It has nothing to do with what life is. Beneath this
bland, this conqueror-image, a great many unadmitted
despairs and confusions, and anguish and unadmitted
crimes and failures hide. To speak in my own person,
as a member of the nation's most oppressed minority,
the oldest oppressed minority, I want to suggest most
seriously that before we can do very much in the way of
clear thinking or clear doing as relates to the minorities
in this country, we must first crack the American image
and find out and deal with what it hides. We cannot discuss the state of our minorities until we first have some
sense of what we are, who we are, what our goals are,
and what we take life to be. The question is not what we
can do now for the hypothetical Mexican, the hypothetical Negro. The question is what we really want out of
life, for ourselves, what we think is real.

Now I think there is a very good reason why the
Negro in this country has been treated for such a long
time in such a cruel way, and some of the reasons are

economic and some of them are political. We have
discussed these reasons without ever coming to any kind
of resolution for a very long time. Some of them are
social, and these reasons are somewhat more important
because they have to do with our social panic, with our
fear of losing status. This really amounts sometimes to
a kind of social paranoia. One cannot afford to lose
status on this peculiar ladder, for the prevailing notion
of American life seems to involve a kind of rung-by-
rung ascension to some hideously desirable state. If
this is one's concept of life, obviously one cannot
afford to slip back one rung. When one slips, one slips
back not a rung but back into chaos and no longer knows
who he is. And this reason, this fear, suggests to me one
of the real reasons for the status of the Negro in this
country. In a way, the Negro tells us where the bottom
is: *because he is there*, and *where* he is, beneath us,
we know where the limits are and how far we must
not fall. We must not fall beneath him. We must never
allow ourselves to fall that low, and I am not trying to
be cynical or sardonic. I think if one examines the
myths which have proliferated in this country concerning the Negro, one discovers beneath these myths a kind
of sleeping terror of some condition which we refuse to
imagine. In a way, if the Negro were not here, we might
be forced to deal within ourselves and our own personalities, with all those vices, all those conundrums,
and all those mysteries with which we have invested the

Negro race. Uncle Tom is, for example, if he is called
uncle, a kind of saint. He is there, he endures, he will
forgive us, and this is a key to that image. But if he is
not uncle, if he is merely Tom, he is a danger to everybody. He will wreak havoc on the countryside. When he
is Uncle Tom he has no sex—when he is Tom, he does—
and this obviously says much more about the people who
invented this myth than it does about the people who
are the object of it.

If you have been watching television lately, I think
this is unendurably clear in the faces of those screaming
people in the South, who are quite incapable of telling
you what it is they are afraid of. They do not really
know what it is they are afraid of, but they know they
are afraid of something, and they are so frightened that
they are nearly out of their minds. And this same fear
obtains on one level or another, to varying degrees,
throughout the entire country. We would never, never
allow Negroes to starve, to grow bitter, and to die in
ghettos all over the country if we were not driven by
some nameless fear that has nothing to do with Negroes.
We would never victimize, as we do, children whose
only crime is color and keep them, as we put it, in their
place. We wouldn't drive Negroes mad as we do by accepting them in ball parks, and on concert stages, but
not in our homes and not in our neighborhoods, and not
in our churches. It is only too clear that even with the
most malevolent will in the world Negroes can never

manage to achieve one-tenth of the harm which we fear. No, it has everything to do with ourselves and this is one of the reasons that for all these generations we have disguised this problem in the most incredible jargon. One of the reasons we are so fond of sociological reports and research and investigational committees is because they hide something. As long as we can deal with the Negro as a kind of statistic, as something to be manipulated, something to be fled from, or something to be given something to, there is something we can avoid, and what we can avoid is what he really, really means to us. The question that still ends these discussions is an extraordinary question: Would you let your sister marry one? The question, by the way, depends on several extraordinary assumptions. First of all it assumes, if I may say so, that I *want* to marry your sister and it also assumes that if I asked your sister to marry me, she would immediately say yes. There is no reason to make either of these assumptions, which are clearly irrational, and the key to why these assumptions are held is not to be found by asking Negroes. The key to why these assumptions are held has something to do with some insecurity in the people who hold them. It is only, after all, too clear that everyone born is going to have a rather difficult time getting through his life. It is only too clear that people fall in love according to some principle that we have not as yet been able to define, to discover or to isolate, and that marriage depends entirely on the two people

involved; so that this objection does not hold water. It
certainly is not justification for segregated schools or for
ghettos or for mobs. I suggest that the role of the Negro
in American life has something to do with our concept of what God is, and from my point of view, this
concept is not big enough. It has got to be made much
bigger than it is because God is, after all, not anybody's
toy. To be with God is really to be involved with some
enormous, overwhelming desire, and joy, and power
which you cannot control, which controls you. I conceive
of my own life as a journey toward something I do not
understand, which in the going toward, makes me better.
I conceive of God, in fact, as a means of liberation and
not a means to control others. Love does not begin and
end the way we seem to think it does. Love is a battle,
love is a war; love is a growing up. No one in the world
—in the entire world—knows more—knows Americans
better or, odd as this may sound, loves them more than
the American Negro. This is because he has had to
watch you, outwit you, deal with you, and bear you, and
sometimes even bleed and die with you, ever since we
got here, that is, since both of us, black and white, got
here—and this is a wedding. Whether I like it or not,
or whether you like it or not, we are bound together
forever. We are part of each other. What is happening
to every Negro in the country at any time is also happening to you. There is no way around this. I am suggesting
that these walls—these artificial walls—which have been

up so long to protect us from something we fear, must come down. I think that what we really have to do is to create a country in which there are no minorities—for the first time in the history of the world. The one thing that all Americans have in common is that they have no other identity apart from the identity which is being achieved on this continent. This is not the English necessity, or the Chinese necessity, or the French necessity, but they are born into a framework which allows them their identity. The necessity of Americans to achieve an identity is a historical and a present personal fact and this is the connection between you and me.

This brings me back, in a way, to where I started. I said that we couldn't talk about minorities until we had talked about majorities, and I also said that majorities had nothing to do with numbers or with power, but with influence, with moral influence, and I want to suggest this: that the majority for which everyone is seeking which must reassess and release us from our past and deal with the present and create standards worthy of what a man may be—this majority is you. No one else can do it. The world is before you and you need not take it or leave it as it was when you came in.

PART TWO

... With Everything On My Mind

9. Notes for a Hypothetical Novel:

An Address

WE'VE BEEN TALKING ABOUT writing for the last two days, which is a very reckless thing to do, so that I shall be absolutely reckless tonight and pretend that I'm writing a novel in your presence. I'm going to ramble on a little tonight about my own past, not as though it were my own past exactly, but as a subject for fiction. I'm doing this in a kind of halting attempt to relate the terms of my experience to yours; and to find out what specific principle, if any, unites us in spite of all the obvious disparities, some of which are superficial and some of which are profound, and most of which are entirely misunderstood. We'll come back to that, in any case, this misunderstanding, I mean, in a minute, but I want to warn you that I'm not pretending to be unbiased. I'm certain that there is something which unites all the Americans in this room,

141

though I can't say what it is. But if I were to meet any one of you in some other country, England, Italy, France, or Spain, it would be at once apparent to everybody else, though it might not be to us, that we had something in common which scarcely any other people, or no other people could really share.

Let's pretend that I want to write a novel concerning the people or some of the people with whom I grew up, and since we are only playing let us pretend it's a very long novel. I want to follow a group of lives almost from the time they open their eyes on the world until some point of resolution, say, marriage, or childbirth, or death. And I want to impose myself on these people as little as possible. That means that I do not want to tell them or the reader what principle their lives illustrate, or what principle is activating their lives, but by examining their lives I hope to be able to make them convey to me and to the reader what their lives mean.

Now I know that this is not altogether possible. I mean that I know that my people are controlled by my point of view and that by the time I begin the novel I have some idea of what I want the novel to do, or to say, or to be. But just the same, whatever my point of view is and whatever my intentions, because I am an American writer my subject and my material inevitably has to be a handful of incoherent people in an incoherent country. And I don't mean incoherent in any light sense, and later on we'll talk about what I mean when I use that word.

Well, who are these people who fill my past and seem to clamor to be expressed? I was born on a very wide avenue in Harlem, and in those days that part of town was called The Hollow and now it's called Junkie's Hollow. The time was the 1920's, and as I was coming into the world there was something going on called The Negro Renaissance; and the most distinguished survivor of that time is Mr. Langston Hughes. This Negro Renaissance is an elegant term which means that white people had then discovered that Negroes could act and write as well as sing and dance and this Renaissance was not destined to last very long. Very shortly there was to be a depression and the artistic Negro, or the noble savage, was to give way to the militant or the new Negro; and I want to point out something in passing which I think is worth our time to look at, which is this: that the country's image of the Negro, which hasn't very much to do with the Negro, has never failed to reflect with a kind of frightening accuracy the state of mind of the country. This was the Jazz Age you will remember. It was the epoch of F. Scott Fitzgerald, Josephine Baker had just gone to France, Mussolini had just come to power in Italy, there was a peculiar man in Germany who was plotting and writing, and the lord knows what Lumumba's mother was thinking. And all of these things and a million more which are now known to the novelist, but not to his people, are to have a terrible effect on their lives.

There's a figure I carry in my mind's eye to this day

and I don't know why. He can't really be the first person
I remember, but he seems to be, apart from my mother
and my father, and this is a man about as old perhaps
as I am now who's coming up our street, very drunk,
falling-down drunk, and it must have been a Saturday
and I was sitting in the window. It must have been winter
because I remember he had a black overcoat on—because his overcoat was open—and he's stumbling past
one of those high, iron railings with spikes on top, and
he falls and he bumps his head against one of these railings, and blood comes down his face, and there are kids
behind him and they're tormenting him and laughing
at him. And that's all I remember and I don't know why.
But I only throw him in to dramatize this fact, that however solemn we writers, or myself, I, may sometimes
sound, or how pontifical I may sometimes seem to be, on
that level from which any genuine work of the imagination springs, I'm really, and we all are, absolutely helpless and ignorant. But this figure is important because
he's going to appear in my novel. He can't be kept out
of it. He occupies too large a place in my imagination.

And then, of course, I remember the church people
because I was practically born in the church, and I seem
to have spent most of the time that I was helpless sitting
on someone's lap in the church and being beaten over
the head whenever I fell asleep, which was usually.
I was frightened of all those brothers and sisters of the
church because they were all powerful, I thought they

were. And I had one ally, my brother, who was a very undependable ally because sometimes I got beaten for things he did and sometimes he got beaten for things I did. But we were united in our hatred for the deacons and the deaconesses and the shouting sisters and of our father. And one of the reasons for this is that we were always hungry and he was always inviting those people over to the house on Sunday for an enormous banquet and we sat next to the icebox in the kitchen watching all those hams, and chickens, and biscuits go down those righteous bellies, which had no bottom.

Now so far, in this hypothetical sketch of an unwritten and probably unwritable novel, so good. From what we've already sketched we can begin to anticipate one of those long, warm, toasty novels. You know, those novels in which the novelist is looking back on himself, absolutely infatuated with himself as a child and everything is in sentimentality. But I think we ought to bring ourselves up short because we don't need another version of *A Tree Grows in Brooklyn* and we can do without another version of *The Heart Is a Lonely Hunter*. This hypothetical book is aiming at something more implacable than that. Because no matter how ridiculous this may sound, that unseen prisoner in Germany is going to have an effect on the lives of these people. Two Italians are going to be executed presently in Boston, there's going to be something called the Scottsboro case which will give the Communist party hideous opportunities. In short, the social realities with which these people, the people I remember, whether they knew it or not, were really contending can't be left out of the novel without falsifying their experience. And—this is very important—this all has something to do with the sight of that tormented, falling down, drunken, bleeding man I mentioned at the beginning. Who is he and what does he mean?

Well, then I remember, principally I remember, the boys and girls in the streets. The boys and girls on the streets, at school, in the church. I remember in the beginning I only knew Negroes except for one Jewish boy, the only white boy in an all-Negro elementary school, a kind of survivor of another day in Harlem, and there was an Italian fruit vendor who lived next door to us who had a son with whom I fought every campaign of the Italian-Ethiopian war. Because, remember that we're projecting a novel, and Harlem is in the course of changing all the time, very soon there won't be any white people there, and this is also going to have some effect on the people in my story.

Well, more people now. There was a boy, a member of our church, and he backslid, which means he achieved a sex life and started smoking cigarettes, and he was therefore rejected from the community in which he had been brought up, because Harlem is also reduced to communities. And I've always believed that one of the reasons he died was because of this rejection. In any case, eighteen months after he was thrown out of the church he was dead of tuberculosis.

And there was a girl, who was a nice girl. She was a niece of one of the deaconesses. In fact, she was my girl. We were very young then, we were going to get married and we were always singing, praying and shouting, and we thought we'd live that way forever. But one day she was picked up in a nightgown on Lenox Avenue screaming and cursing and they carried her away to an institution where she still may be.

And by this time I was a big boy, and there were the friends of my brothers, my younger brothers and sisters. And I had danced to Duke Ellington, but they were dancing to Charlie Parker; and I had learned how to drink gin and whisky, but they were involved with marijuana and the needle. I will not really insist upon continuing this roster. I have not known many survivors. I know mainly about disaster, but then I want to remind you again of that man I mentioned in the beginning, who haunts the imagination of this novelist. The imagination of a novelist has everything to do with what happens to his material.

Now, we're a little beyond the territory of Betty Smith and Carson McCullers, but we are not quite beyond the territory of James T. Farrell or Richard Wright. Let's go a little bit farther. By and by I left Harlem. I left all those deaconesses, all those sisters, and all those churches, and all those tambourines, and I entered or anyway I encountered the white world. Now this white world which I was just encountering was, just the same, one of the forces that had been controlling me from the time I opened my eyes on the world. For it is important to ask, I think, where did these people I'm talking about come from and where did they get their peculiar school of ethics? What was its origin? What did it mean to them? What did it come out of? What function did it serve and why was it happening here? And why were they living where they were and what was it doing to them? All these things which sociologists think they can find out and haven't managed to do, which no chart can tell us. People are not, though in our age we seem to think so, endlessly manipulable. We think that once one has discovered that thirty thousand, let us say, Negroes, Chinese or Puerto Ricans or whatever have syphilis or don't, or are unemployed or not, that we've discovered something about the Negroes, Chinese or Puerto Ricans. But in fact, this is not so. In fact, we've discovered nothing very useful because people cannot be handled in that way.

Anyway, in the beginning I thought that the white world was very different from the world I was moving out of and I turned out to be entirely wrong. It seemed different. It seemed safer, at least the white people seemed safer. It seemed cleaner, it seemed more polite, and, of course, it seemed much richer from the material point of view. But I didn't meet anyone in that world

who didn't suffer from the very same affliction that all
the people I had fled from suffered from and that was
that they didn't know who they were. They wanted to be
something that they were not. And very shortly I didn't
know who I was, either. I could not be certain whether I
was really rich or really poor, really black or really
white, really male or really female, really talented or a
fraud, really strong or merely stubborn. In short, I had
become an American. I had stepped into, I had walked
right into, as I inevitably had to do, the bottomless confusion which is both public and private, of the American
republic.

Now we've brought this hypothetical hero to this
place, now what are we going to do with him, what does
all of this mean, what can we make it mean? What's the
thread that unites all these peculiar and disparate lives,
whether it's from Idaho to San Francisco, from Idaho to
New York, from Boston to Birmingham? Because there
is something that unites all of these people and places.
What does it mean to be an American? What nerve is
pressed in you or me when we hear this word?

Earlier I spoke about the disparities and I said I was
going to try and give an example of what I meant. Now
the most obvious thing that would seem to divide me
from the rest of my countrymen is the fact of color.
The fact of color has a relevance objectively and some
relevance in some other way, some emotional relevance
and not only for the South. I mean that it persists as a

problem in American life because it means something, it fulfills something in the American personality. It is here because the Americans in some peculiar way believe or think they need it. Maybe we can find out what it is that this problem fulfills in the American personality, what it corroborates and in what way this peculiar thing, until today, helps Americans to feel safe.

When I spoke about incoherence I said I'd try to tell you what I meant by that word. It's a kind of incoherence that occurs, let us say, when I am frightened, I am absolutely frightened to death, and there's something which is happening or about to happen that I don't want to face, or, let us say, which is an even better example, that I have a friend who has just murdered his mother and put her in the closet and I know it, but we're not going to talk about it. Now this means very shortly since, after all, I know the corpse is in the closet, and he knows I know it, and we're sitting around having a few drinks and trying to be buddy-buddy together, that very shortly, we can't talk about anything because we can't talk about that. No matter what I say I may inadvertently stumble on this corpse. And this incoherence which seems to afflict this country is analogous to that. I mean that in order to have a conversation with someone you have to reveal yourself. In order to have a real relationship with somebody you have got to take the risk of being thought, God forbid, "an oddball." You know, you have to take a chance which in some

peculiar way we don't seem willing to take. And this is
very serious in that it is not so much a writer's problem,
that is to say, I don't want to talk about it from the point
of view of a writer's problem, because, after all, you
didn't ask me to become a writer, but it seems to me
that the situation of the writer in this country is symp-
tomatic and reveals, says something, very terrifying
about this country. If I were writing hypothetically
about a Frenchman I would have in a way a frame of
reference and a point of view and in fact it is easier to
write about Frenchmen, comparatively speaking, because they interest me so much less. But to try to deal
with the American experience, that is to say to deal with
this enormous incoherence, these enormous puddings,
this shapeless thing, to try and make an American, well
listen to them, and try to put that on a page. The truth
about dialogue, for example, or the technical side of it,
is that you try and make people say what they would say
if they could and then you sort of dress it up to look like
speech. That is to say that it's really an absolute height,
people don't ever talk the way they talk in novels, but
I've got to make you believe they do because I can't
possibly do a tape recording.

But to try and find out what Americans mean is almost impossible because there are so many things they
do not want to face. And not only the Negro thing which
is simply the most obvious and perhaps the simplest
example, but on the level of private life which is after

all where we have to get to in order to write about anything and also the level we have to get to in order to live,
it seems to me that the myth, the illusion, that this is a
free country, for example, is disastrous. Let me point
out to you that freedom is not something that anybody
can be given; freedom is something people take and
people are as free as they want to be. One hasn't got to
have an enormous military machine in order to be un-
free when it's simpler to be asleep, when it's simpler to
be apathetic, when it's simpler, in fact, not to want to be
free, to think that something else is more important. And
I'm not using freedom now so much in a political sense
as I'm using it in a personal sense. It seems to me that
the confusion is revealed, for example, in those dreadful
speeches by Eisenhower, those incredible speeches by
Nixon, they sound very much, after all, like the jargon
of the Beat generation, that is, in terms of clarity. Not a
pin to be chosen between them, both levels, that is, the
highest level presumably, the administration in Washington, and the lowest level in our national life, the
people who are called "beatniks" are both involved in
saying that something which is really on their heels does
not exist. Jack Kerouac says "Holy, holy" and we say
Red China does not exist. But it really does. I'm simply
trying to point out that it's the symptom of the same
madness.

Now, in some way, somehow, the problem the
writer has which is, after all, his problem and perhaps

not yours is somehow to unite these things, to find the
terms of our connection, without which we will perish.
The importance of a writer is continuous; I think it's
socially debatable and usually socially not terribly
rewarding, but that's not the point; his importance, I
think, is that he is here to describe things which other
people are too busy to describe. It is a function, let's
face it, it's a special function. There is no democracy on this level. It's a very difficult thing to do, it's a
very special thing to do and people who do it cannot by
that token do many other things. But their importance is,
and the importance of writers in this country now is this,
that this country is yet to be discovered in any real sense.
There is an illusion about America, a myth about
America to which we are clinging which has nothing to
do with the lives we lead and I don't believe that anybody in this country who has really thought about it or
really almost anybody who has been brought up against
it—and almost all of us have one way or another—this
collision between one's image of oneself and what one
actually is is always very painful and there are two
things you can do about it, you can meet the collision
head-on and try and become what you really are or you
can retreat and try to remain what you thought you
were, which is a fantasy, in which you will certainly
perish. Now, I don't want to keep you any longer. But
I'd like to leave you with this, I think we have some idea
about reality which is not quite true. Without having

anything whatever against Cadillacs, refrigerators or all the paraphernalia of American life, I yet suspect that there is something much more important and much more real which produces the Cadillac, refrigerator, atom bomb, and what produces it, after all, is something which we don't seem to want to look at, and that is the person. A country is only as good—I don't care now about the Constitution and the laws, at the moment let us leave these things aside—a country is only as strong as the people who make it up and the country turns into what the people want it to become. Now, this country is going to be transformed. It will not be transformed by an act of God, but by all of us, by you and me. I don't believe any longer that we can afford to say that it is entirely out of our hands. We made the world we're living in and we have to make it over.

10. The Male Prison

THERE IS SOMETHING IMMENSELY humbling in this last document [*Madeleine* by André Gide] from the hand of a writer whose elaborately graceful fiction very often impressed me as simply cold, solemn and irritatingly pious, and whose precise memoirs made me accuse him of the most exasperating egocentricity. He does not, to be sure, emerge in *Madeleine* as being less egocentric; but one is compelled to see this egocentricity as one of the conditions of his life and one of the elements of his pain. Nor can I claim that reading *Madeleine* has caused me to re-evaluate his fiction (though I care more now for *The Immoralist* than I did when I read it several years ago); it has only made me feel that such a re-evaluation must be made. For, whatever Gide's shortcomings may have been, few writers of our time can equal his devotion to a very high ideal.

It seems to me now that the two things which contrib-

uted most heavily to my dislike of Gide—or, rather, to
the discomfort he caused me to feel—were his Protestantism and his homosexuality. It was clear to me that he
had not got over his Protestantism and that he had not
come to terms with his nature. (For I believed at one
time—rather oddly, considering the examples by which
I was surrounded, to say nothing of the spectacle I myself presented—that people *did* "get over" their earliest
impressions and that "coming to terms" with oneself
simply demanded a slightly more protracted stiffening
of the will.) It was his Protestantism, I felt, which made
him so pious, which invested all of his work with the air
of an endless winter, and which made it so difficult for
me to care what happened to any of his people.

And his homosexuality, I felt, was his own affair
which he ought to have kept hidden from us, or, if he
needed to be so explicit, he ought at least to have managed to be a little more scientific—whatever, in the do-
main of morals, that word may mean—less illogical,
less romantic. He ought to have leaned less heavily on
the examples of dead, great men, of vanished cultures,
and he ought certainly to have known that the examples
provided by natural history do not go far toward illuminating the physical, psychological and moral complexities faced by men. If he were going to talk about
homosexuality at all, he ought, in a word, to have
sounded a little less *disturbed*.

This is not the place and I am certainly not the man

to assess the work of André Gide. Moreover, I confess that a great deal of what I felt concerning his work I still feel. And that argument, for example, as to whether or not homosexuality is natural seems to me completely pointless—pointless because I really do not see what difference the answer makes. It seems clear, in any case, at least in the world we know, that no matter what encyclopedias of physiological and scientific knowledge are brought to bear the answer never can be Yes. And one of the reasons for this is that it would rob the normal—who are simply the many—of their very necessary sense of security and order, of their sense, perhaps, that the race is and should be devoted to outwitting oblivion—and will surely manage to do so.

But there are a great many ways of outwitting oblivion, and to ask whether or not homosexuality is natural is really like asking whether or not it was natural for Socrates to swallow hemlock, whether or not it was natural for St. Paul to suffer for the Gospel, whether or not it was natural for the Germans to send upwards of six million people to an extremely twentieth-century death. It does not seem to me that nature helps us very much when we need illumination in human affairs. I am certainly convinced that it is one of the greatest impulses of mankind to arrive at something higher than a natural state. How to be natural does not seem to me to be a problem —quite the contrary. The great problem is how to be— in the best sense of that kaleidoscopic word—a man.

This problem was at the heart of all Gide's anguish, and it proved itself, like most real problems, to be insoluble. He died, as it were, with the teeth of this problem still buried in his throat. What one learns from *Madeleine* is what it cost him, in terms of unceasing agony, to live with this problem at all. Of what it cost her, his wife, it is scarcely possible to conjecture. But she was not so much a victim of Gide's sexual nature—homosexuals do not choose women for their victims, nor is the difficulty of becoming a victim so great for a woman that she is compelled to turn to homosexuals for this—as she was a victim of his overwhelming guilt, which connected, it would seem, and most unluckily, with her own guilt and shame.

If this meant, as Gide says, that "the spiritual force of my love [for Madeleine] inhibited all carnal desire," it also meant that some corresponding inhibition in her prevented her from seeking carnal satisfaction elsewhere. And if there is scarcely any suggestion through out this appalling letter that Gide ever really understood that he had married a woman or that he had any apprehension of what a woman was, neither is there any suggestion that she ever, in any way, insisted on or was able to believe in her womanhood and its right to flower.

Her most definite and also most desperate act is the burning of his letters—and the anguish this cost her, and the fact that in this burning she expressed what surely must have seemed to her life's monumental fail-

ure and waste, Gide characteristically (indeed, one may
say, necessarily) cannot enter into and cannot understand. "They were my most precious belongings," she
tells him, and perhaps he cannot be blamed for protecting himself against the knife of this dreadful conjugal
confession. But: "It is the best of me that disappears,"
he tells us, *and it will no longer counterbalance the
worst.*" (Italics mine.) He had entrusted, as it were, to
her his purity, that part of him that was not carnal; and
it is quite clear that, though he suspected it, he could
not face the fact that it was only when her purity
ended that her life could begin, that the key to her liberation was in his hands.

But if he had ever turned that key madness and despair would have followed for him, his world would have
turned completely dark, the string connecting him to
heaven would have been cut. And this is because then he
could no longer have loved Madeleine as an ideal, as
Emanuele, God-with-us, but would have been compelled
to love her as a woman, which he could not have done
except physically. And then he would have had to hate
her, and at that moment those gates which, as it seemed
to him, held him back from utter corruption would have
been opened. He loved her as a woman, indeed, only in
the sense that no man could have held the place in Gide's
dark sky which was held by Madeleine. She was his
Heaven who would forgive him for his Hell and help
him to endure it. As indeed she was and, in the strangest

way possible, did—by allowing him to feel guilty about *her* instead of the boys on the *Piazza d'Espagne*—with the result that, in Gide's work, both his Heaven and his Hell suffer from a certain lack of urgency.

Gide's relations with Madeleine place his relations with men in rather a bleak light. Since he clearly could not forgive himself for his anomaly, he must certainly have despised them—which almost certainly explains the fascination felt by Gide and so many of his heroes for countries like North Africa. It is not necessary to despise people who are one's inferiors—whose inferiority, by the way, is amply demonstrated by the fact that they appear to relish, without guilt, their sensuality.

It is possible, as it were, to have one's pleasure without paying for it. But to have one's pleasure without paying for it is precisely the way to find oneself reduced to a search for pleasure which grows steadily more desperate and more grotesque. It does not take long, after all, to discover that sex is only sex, that there are few things on earth more futile or more deadening than a meaningless round of conquests. The really horrible thing about the phenomenon of present-day homosexuality, the horrible thing which lies curled like a worm at the heart of Gide's trouble and his work and the reason that he so clung to Madeleine, is that today's unlucky deviate can only save himself by the most tremendous exertion of all his forces from falling into an underworld in which he never meets either men or women, where it is impossible to have either a lover or a friend, where the possibility of genuine human involvement has altogether ceased. When this possibility has ceased, so has the possibility of growth.

And, again: It is one of the facts of life that there are two sexes, which fact has given the world most of its beauty, cost it not a little of its anguish, and contains the hope and glory of the world. And it is with this fact, which might better perhaps be called a mystery, that every human being born must find some way to live. For, no matter what demons drive them, men cannot live without women and women cannot live without men. And this is what is most clearly conveyed in the agony of Gide's last journal. However little he was able to understand it, or, more important perhaps, take upon himself the responsibility for it, Madeleine kept open for him a kind of door of hope, of possibility, the possibility of entering into communion with another sex. This door, which is the door to life and air and freedom from the tyranny of one's own personality, *must* be kept open, and none feel this more keenly than those on whom the door is perpetually threatening or has already seemed to close.

Gide's dilemma, his wrestling, his peculiar, notable and extremely valuable failure testify—which should not seem odd—to a powerful masculinity and also to the fact that he found no way to escape the prison of that masculinity. And the fact that he endured this

prison with such dignity is precisely what ought to
humble us all, living as we do in a time and country
where communion between the sexes has become so
sorely threatened that we depend more and more on
the strident exploitation of externals, as, for example,
the breasts of Hollywood glamour girls and the mindless
grunting and swaggering of Hollywood he-men.

It is important to remember that the prison in which
Gide struggled is not really so unique as it would certainly comfort us to believe, is not very different from
the prison inhabited by, say, the heroes of Mickey Spil-
lane. Neither can they get through to women, which is
the only reason their muscles, their fists and their
tommy guns have acquired such fantastic importance. It
is worth observing, too, that when men can no longer
love women they also cease to love or respect or trust
each other, which makes their isolation complete. Nothing is more dangerous than this isolation, for men will
commit any crimes whatever rather than endure it. We
ought, for our own sakes, to be humbled by Gide's confession as he was humbled by his pain and make the
generous effort to understand that his sorrow was not
different from the sorrow of all men born. For, if we do
not learn this humility, we may very well be strangled
by a most petulant and unmasculine pride.

11. The Northern Protestant

I ALREADY KNEW THAT BERGMAN had just completed one movie, was mixing the sound for it, and was scheduled to begin another almost at once. When I called the Filmstaden, he himself, incredibly enough, came to the phone. He sounded tired but very pleasant, and told me he could see me if I came at once.

The Filmstaden is in a suburb of Stockholm called Rasunda, and is the headquarters of the Svensk Filmindustri, which is one of the oldest movie companies in the world. It was here that Victor Sjöström made those remarkable movies which, eventually (under the name of Victor Seastrom) carried him—briefly—to the arid plains of Hollywood. Here Mauritz Stiller directed *The Legend of Gösta Berling*, after which he and the star thus discovered, Garbo, also took themselves west—a disastrous move for Stiller and not, as it was to turn

out, altogether the most fruitful move, artistically anyway, that Garbo could have made. Ingrid Bergman left
here in 1939. (She is not related to Ingmar Bergman.)
The Svensk Filmindustri is proud of these alumni, but
they are prouder of no one, at the moment, than they
are of Ingmar Bergman, whose films have placed the
Swedish film industry back on the international map.
And yet, on the whole, they take a remarkably steady
view of the Bergman vogue. They realize that it *is* a
vogue, they are bracing themselves for the inevitable reaction, and they hope that Bergman is doing the same.
He is neither as great nor as limited as the current hue
and cry suggests. But he is one of the very few genuine
artists now working in films.

He is also, beyond doubt, the freest. Not for him the
necessity of working on a shoestring, with unpaid performers, as has been the case with many of the younger
French directors. He is backed by a film company;
Swedish film companies usually own their laboratories,
studios, rental distribution services, and theaters. If
they did not they could scarcely afford to make movies
at all, movies being more highly taxed in this tiny
country than anywhere else in the world—except Den-
mark—and 60 per cent of the playing time in these
company-owned theaters being taken up by foreign
films. Nor can the Swedish film industry possibly support anything resembling the American star system.
This is healthy for the performers, who never have to

sit idly by for a couple of years, waiting for a fat
part, and who are able to develop a range and flexibility
rarely permitted even to the most gifted of our stars.
And, of course, it's fine for Bergman because he is
absolutely free to choose his own performers: if he
wishes to work, say, with Geraldine Page, studio pressure will not force him into extracting a performance
from Kim Novak. If it were not for this freedom we
would almost certainly never have heard of Ingmar
Bergman. Most of his twenty-odd movies were not suc-
cessful when they were made, nor are they today his
company's biggest money-makers. (His vogue has
changed this somewhat, but, as I say, no one expects this
vogue to last.) "He wins the prizes and brings us the
prestige," was the comment of one of his co-workers,
"but it's So-and-So and So-and-So—" and here he
named two very popular Swedish directors—"who can
be counted on to bring in the money."

I arrived at the Filmstaden a little early; Bergman
was still busy and would be a little late in meeting me,
I was told. I was taken into his office to wait for him. I
welcomed the opportunity of seeing the office without the
man.

It is a very small office, most of it taken up by a desk.
The desk is placed smack in front of the window—not
that it could have been placed anywhere else; this window looks out on the daylight landscape of Bergman's

movies. It was gray and glaring the first day I was there, dry and fiery. Leaves kept falling from the trees, each silent descent bringing a little closer the long, dark, Swedish winter. The forest Bergman's characters are always traversing is outside this window and the ominous carriage from which they have yet to escape is still among the properties. I realized, with a small shock, that the landscape of Bergman's mind was simply the landscape in which he had grown up.

On the desk were papers, folders, a few books, all very neatly arranged. Squeezed between the desk and the wall was a spartan cot; a brown leather jacket and a brown knitted cap were lying on it. The visitor's chair in which I sat was placed at an angle to the door, which proximity, each time that I was there, led to much bumping and scraping and smiling exchanges in Esperanto. On the wall were three photographs of Charlie Chaplin and one of Victor Sjöström.

Eventually, he came in, bareheaded, wearing a sweater, a tall man, economically, intimidatingly lean. He must have been the gawkiest of adolescents, his arms and legs still seeming to be very loosely anchored; something in his good-natured, self-possessed directness suggests that he would also have been among the most belligerently opinionated: by no means an easy man to deal with, in any sense, any relationship whatever, there being about him the evangelical distance of someone possessed by a vision. This extremely dangerous quality—authority—has never failed to incite the hostility of the many. And I got the impression that Bergman was in the habit of saying what he felt because he knew that scarcely anyone was listening.

He suggested tea, partly, I think, to give both of us time to become easier with each other, but also because he really needed a cup of tea before going back to work. We walked out of the office and down the road to the canteen.

I had arrived in Stockholm with what turned out to be the "flu" and I kept coughing and sneezing and wiping my eyes. After a while Bergman began to look at me worriedly and said that I sounded very ill.

I hadn't come there to talk about my health and I tried to change the subject. But I was shortly to learn that any subject changing to be done around Bergman is done by Bergman. He was not to be sidetracked.

"Can I do anything for you?" he persisted; and when I did not answer, being both touched and irritated by his question, he smiled and said, "You haven't to be shy. I know what it is like to be ill and alone in a strange city."

It was a hideously, an inevitably self-conscious gesture and yet it touched and disarmed me. I know that his concern, at bottom, had very little to do with me. It had to do with his memories of himself and it expressed his determination never to be guilty of the world's indifference.

He turned and looked out of the canteen window, at the brilliant October trees and the glaring sky, for a few seconds and then turned back to me.

"Well," he asked me, with a small laugh, "are you for me or against me?"

I did not know how to answer this question right away and he continued, "I don't care if you are or not. Well, that's not true. Naturally, I prefer—I would be happier —if you were *for* me. But I have to know."

I told him I was for him, which might, indeed, turn out to be my principal difficulty in writing about him. I had seen many of his movies—but did not intend to try to see them all—and I felt identified, in some way, with what I felt he was trying to do. What he saw when he looked at the world did not seem very different from what *I* saw. Some of his films seemed rather cold to me, somewhat too deliberate. For example, I had possibly heard too much about *The Seventh Seal* before seeing it, but it had impressed me less than some of the others.

"I cannot discuss that film," he said abruptly, and again turned to look out of the window. "I had to do it. I had to be free of that argument, those questions." He looked at me. "It's the same for you when you write a book? You just do it because you must and then, when you have done it, you are relieved, no?"

He laughed and poured some tea. He had made it sound as though we were two urchins playing a deadly

and delightful game which must be kept a secret from
our elders.

"Those questions?"

"Oh. God and the Devil. Life and Death. Good and
Evil." He smiled. *"Those* questions."

I wanted to suggest that his being a pastor's son contributed not a little to his dark preoccupations. But I
did not quite know how to go about digging into his
private life. I hoped that we would be able to do it by
way of the movies.

I began with: "The question of love seems to occupy
you a great deal, too."

I don't doubt that it occupies you, too, was what he
seemed to be thinking, but he only said, mildly, "Yes."
Then, before I could put it another way, "You may find
it a bit hard to talk to me. I really do not see much
point in talking about my past work. And I cannot talk
about work I haven't done yet."

I mentioned his great preoccupation with egotism,
so many of his people being centered on themselves,
necessarily, and disastrously: Vogler in *The Magician*,
Isak Borg in *Wild Strawberries*, the ballerina in *Summer Interlude*.

"I am very fond of *Summer Interlude*," he said. "It is
my favorite movie.

"I don't mean," he added, "that it's my best. I don't
know which movie is my best."

Summer Interlude was made in 1950. It is probably

not Bergman's best movie—I would give that place to
the movie which has been shown in the States as *The
Naked Night*—but it is certainly among the most moving. Its strength lies in its portrait of the ballerina, un-
cannily precise and truthful, and in its perception of the
nature of first love, which first seems to open the universe to us and then seems to lock us out of it. It is one
of the group of films—including *The Waiting Women,
Smiles of a Summer Night,* and *Brink of Life*—which
have a woman, or women, at their center and in which
the men, generally, are rather shadowy. But all the
Bergman themes are in it: his preoccupation with time
and the inevitability of death, the comedy of human
entanglements, the nature of illusion, the nature of egotism, the price of art. These themes also run through
the movies which have at their center a man: *The
Naked Night* (which should really be called *The Clown's
Evening*), *Wild Strawberries, The Face, The Seventh
Seal.* In only one of these movies—*The Face*—is the
male-female relation affirmed from the male point of
view; as being, that is, a source of strength for the man.
In the movies concerned with women, the male-female
relation succeeds only through the passion, wit, or patience of the woman and depends on how astutely she
is able to manipulate the male conceit. *The Naked Night*
is the most blackly ambivalent of Bergman's films—
and surely one of the most brutally erotic movies ever
made—but it is essentially a study of the masculine

helplessness before the female force. *Wild Strawberries*
is inferior to it, I think, being afflicted with a verbal
and visual rhetoric which is Bergman's most annoying
characteristic. But the terrible assessments that the old
Professor is forced to make in it prove that he is not
merely the victim of his women: he is responsible for
what his women have become.

We soon switched from Bergman's movies to the subject of Stockholm.

"It is not a city at all," he said, with intensity. "It is
ridiculous of it to think of itself as a city. It is simply a
rather larger village, set in the middle of some forests
and some lakes. You wonder what it thinks it is doing
there, looking so important."

I was to encounter in many other people this curious
resistance to the idea that Stockholm could possibly
become a city. It certainly seemed to be trying to become a city as fast as it knew how, which is, indeed, the
natural and inevitable fate of any nation's principal com-
mercial and cultural clearing house. But for Bergman,
who is forty-one, and for people who are considerably
younger, Stockholm seems always to have had the aspect of a village. They do not look forward to seeing it
change. Here, as in other European towns and cities,
people can be heard bitterly complaining about the
"Americanization" which is taking place.

This "Americanization," so far as I could learn,
refers largely to the fact that more and more people

are leaving the countryside and moving into Stockholm. Stockholm is not prepared to receive these people, and the inevitable social tensions result, from housing problems to juvenile delinquency. Of course, there are juke boxes grinding out the inevitable rock-and-roll tunes, and there are, too, a few jazz joints which fail, quite, to remind one of anything in the States. And the ghost— one is tempted to call it the effigy—of the late James Dean, complete with uniform, masochistic girl friend, motorcycle, or (hideously painted) car, has made its appearance on the streets of Stockholm. These do not frighten me nearly as much as do the originals in New York, since they have yet to achieve the authentic American bewilderment or the inimitable American snarl. I ought to add, perhaps, that the American Negro remains, for them, a kind of *monstre sacré*, which proves, if anything does, how little they know of the phenomena which they feel compelled to imitate. They are unlike their American models in many ways: for example, they are not suffering from a lack of order but from an excess of it. Sexually, they are not drowning in taboos; they are anxious, on the contrary, to establish one or two.

But the people in Stockholm are right to be frightened. It is not Stockholm's becoming a city which frightens them. What frightens them is that the pressures under which everyone in this century lives are destroying the old simplicities. This is almost always what peo-

ple really mean when they speak of Americanization. It
is an epithet which is used to mask the fact that the entire
social and moral structure that they have built is proving to be absolutely inadequate to the demands now
being placed on it. The old cannot imagine a new one,
or create it. The young have no confidence in the old;
lacking which, they cannot find any standards in themselves by which to live. The most serious result of such
a chaos, though it may not seem to be, is the death of
love. I do not mean merely the bankruptcy of the concept of romantic love—it is entirely possible that this
concept has had its day—but the breakdown of communication between the sexes.

Bergman talked a little about the early stages of his
career. He came to the Filmstaden in 1944, when he
wrote the script for *Torment*. This was a very promising
beginning. But promising beginnings do not mean much,
especially in the movies. Promise, anyway, was never
what Bergman lacked. He lacked flexibility. Neither he
nor anyone else I talked to suggested that he has since
acquired much of this quality; and since he was young
and profoundly ambitious and thoroughly untried, he
lacked confidence. This lack he disguised by tantrums so
violent that they are still talked about at the Filmstaden
today. His exasperating allergies extended to such things
as refusing to work with a carpenter, say, to whom he
had never spoken but whose face he disliked. He has

been known, upon finding guests at his home, to hide himself in the bathroom until they left. Many of these people never returned and it is hard, of course, to blame them. Nor was he, at this time in his life, particularly respectful of the feelings of his friends.

"He's improved," said a woman who has been working with him for the last several years, "but he was impossible. He could say the most terrible things, he could make you wish you were dead. Especially if you were a woman."

She reflected. "Then, later, he would come and apologize. One just had to accept it, that's all."

He was referred to in those days, without affection as "the young one" or "the kid" or "the demon director." An American property whose movies, in spite of all this temperament, made no money at the box office, would have suffered, at best, the fate of Orson Welles. But Bergman went on working, as screen writer and director in films and as a director on the stage.

"I was an actor for a while," he says, "a terribly bad actor. But it taught me much."

It probably taught him a great deal about how to handle actors, which is one of his great gifts.

He directed plays for the municipal theaters of Hälsingborg, Göteborg, and Malmö, and is now working—or will be as soon as he completes his present film schedule —for the Royal Dramatic Theatre of Stockholm.

Some of the people I met told me that his work on

stage is even more exciting than his work in films. They were the same people, usually, who were most concerned for Bergman's future when his present vogue ends. It was as though they were giving him an ace in the hole.

I did not interrogate Bergman on this point, but his record suggests that he is more attracted to films than to the theater. It would seem, too, that the theater very often operates for him as a kind of prolonged rehearsal or preparation for a film already embryonic in his consciousness. This is almost certainly the case with at least two of his theatrical productions. In 1954, he directed, for the municipal theater of Malmö, Franz Lehár's *The Merry Widow*. The next year he wrote and directed the elaborate period comedy, *Smiles of a Summer Night*, which beautifully utilizes—for Bergman's rather savage purposes—the atmosphere of romantic light opera. In 1956, he published his play *A Medieval Fresco*. This play was not produced, but it forms the basis for *The Seventh Seal*, which he wrote and directed the same year. It is safe, I think, to assume that the play will now never be produced, at least not by Bergman.

He has had many offers, of course, to work in other countries. I asked him if he had considered taking any of them.

He looked out of the window again. "I am home here," he said. "It took me a long time, but now I have all my instruments—everything—where I want them. I know my crew, my crew knows me, I know my actors."

I watched him. Something in me, inevitably, envied him for being able to love his home so directly and for being able to stay at home and work. And, in another way, rather to my surprise, I envied him not at all. Everything in a life depends on how that life accepts its limits: it would have been like envying him his language.

"If I were a violinist," he said after a while, "and I were invited to play in Paris—well, if the condition was that I could not bring my own violin but would have to play a French one—well, then, I could not go." He made a quick gesture toward the window. "This is my violin."

It was getting late. I had the feeling that I should be leaving, though he had not made any such suggestion. We got around to talking about *The Magician.*

"It doesn't have anything to do with hypnotism, does it?" I asked him.

"No. No, of course not."

"Then it's a joke. A long, elaborate metaphor for the condition of the artist—I mean, any time, anywhere, all the time—"

He laughed in much the same conspiratorial way he had laughed when talking about his reasons for doing *The Seventh Seal.* "Well, yes. He is always on the very edge of disaster, he is always on the very edge of great things. Always. Isn't it so? It is his element, like water is the element for the fish."

People had been interrupting us from the moment we

sat down, and now someone arrived who clearly intended to take Bergman away with him. We made a date to meet early in the coming week. Bergman stood with me until my cab came and told the driver where I lived. I watched him, tall, bare-headed, and fearfully determined, as he walked away. I thought how there was something in the weird, mad, Northern Protestantism which reminded me of the visions of the black preachers of my childhood.

One of the movies which has made the most profound impression on Bergman is Victor Sjöström's *The Phantom Carriage*. It is based on a novel by Selma Lagerlöf which I have not read—and which, as a novel, I cannot imagine. But it makes great sense as a Northern fable; it has the atmosphere of a tale which has been handed down, for generations, from father to son. The premise of the movie is that whoever dies, in his sins, on New Year's Eve must drive Death's chariot throughout the coming year. The story that the movie tells is how a sinner—beautifully played by Sjöström himself —outwits Death. He outwits Death by virtue, virtue in the biblical, or, rather, in the New Testament sense: he outwits Death by opposing to this anonymous force his weak and ineradicable humanity.

Now this is, of course, precisely the story that Bergman is telling in *The Seventh Seal*. He has managed to utilize the old framework, the old saga, to speak of our condition in the world today and the way in which this loveless and ominous condition can be transcended. This ancient saga is part of his personal past and one of the keys to the people who produced him.

Since I had been so struck by what seemed to be our similarities, I amused myself, on the ride back into town, by projecting a movie, which, if I were a movie-maker, would occupy, among my own productions, the place *The Seventh Seal* holds among Bergman's. I did not have, to hold my films together, the Northern sagas; but I had the Southern music. From the African tom-toms, to Congo Square, to New Orleans, to Harlem—and, finally, all the way to Stockholm, and the European sectors of African towns. My film would begin with slaves, boarding the good ship *Jesus:* a white ship, on a dark sea, with masters as white as the sails of their ships, and slaves as black as the ocean. There would be one intransigent slave, an eternal figure, destined to appear, and to be put to death in every generation. In the hold of the slave ship, he would be a witch-doctor or a chief or a prince or a singer; and he would die, be hurled into the ocean, for protecting a black woman. Who would bear his child, however, and this child would lead a slave insurrection; and be hanged. During the Reconstruction, he would be murdered upon leaving Congress. He would be a returning soldier during the first World War, and be buried alive; and then, during the Depression, he would become a jazz musician, and go mad. Which would bring him up to our own

day—what would his fate be now? What would I en-
title this grim and vengeful fantasy? What would be
happening, during all this time, to the descendants of
the masters? It did not seem likely, after all, that I
would ever be able to make of my past, on film, what
Bergman had been able to make of his. In some ways,
his past is easier to deal with: it was, at once, more
remote and more present. Perhaps what divided the
black Protestant from the white one was the nature of
my still unwieldy, unaccepted bitterness. My hero, now,
my tragic hero, would probably be a junkie—which,
certainly, in one way, suggested the distance covered by
America's dark generations. But it was in only one way,
it was not the whole story; and it then occurred to me
that my bitterness might be turned to good account if I
should dare to envision the tragic hero for whom I
was searching—as myself. All art is a kind of confession,
more or less oblique. All artists, if they are to survive,
are forced, at last, to tell the whole story, to vomit the
anguish up. All of it, the literal and the fanciful. Bergman's authority seemed, then, to come from the fact
that he was reconciled to this arduous, delicate, and dis-
ciplined self-exposure.

Bergman and his father had not got on well when
Bergman was young.

"But how do you get along now?" I had asked him.

"Oh, now," he said, "we get on very well. I go to
see him often."

I told him that I envied him. He smiled and said, "Oh, it is always like that—when such a battle is over, fathers and sons can be friends."

I did not say that such a reconciliation had probably a great deal to do with one's attitude toward one's past, and the uses to which one could put it. But I now began to feel, as I saw my hotel glaring up out of the Stockholm gloom, that what was lacking in my movie was the American despair, the search, in our country for authority. The blue-jeaned boys on the Stockholm streets were really imitations, so far; but the streets of my native city were filled with youngsters searching desperately for the limits which would tell them who they were, and create for them a challenge to which they could rise. What would a Bergman make of the American confusion? How would he handle a love story occurring in New York?

12. Alas, Poor Richard

I.   Eight Men

UNLESS A WRITER IS EXTREMELY old when he dies, in which case he has probably become a neglected institution, his death must always seem untimely. This is because a real writer is always shifting and changing and searching. The world has many labels for him, of which the most treacherous is the label of Success. But the man behind the label knows defeat far more intimately than he knows triumph. He can never be absolutely certain that he has achieved his intention.

This tension and authority—the authority of the frequently defeated—are in the writer's work, and cause one to feel that, at the moment of his death, he was approaching his greatest achievements. I should think that guilt plays some part in this reaction, as well as a certain unadmitted relief. Guilt, because of our failure in a relationship, because it is extremely difficult to deal with writers as people. Writers are said to be extremely egotistical and demanding, and they are indeed, but that does not distinguish them from anyone else. What distinguishes them is what James once described as a kind of "holy stupidity." The writer's greed is appalling. He wants, or seems to want, everything and practically everybody; in another sense, and at the same time, he needs no one at all; and families, friends, and lovers find this extremely hard to take. While he is alive, his work is fatally entangled with his personal fortunes and misfortunes, his personality, and the social facts and attitudes of his time. The unadmitted relief, then, of which I spoke has to do with a certain drop in the intensity of our bewilderment, for the baffling creator no longer stands between us and his works.

He does not, but many other things do, above all our own preoccupations. In the case of Richard Wright, dead in Paris at fifty-two, the fact that he worked during a bewildering and demoralizing era in Western history makes a proper assessment of his work more difficult. In *Eight Men*, the earliest story, "The Man Who Saw the Flood," takes place in the deep South and was first published in 1937. One of the two previously unpublished stories in the book, "Man, God Ain't Like That," begins in Africa, achieves its hideous resolution in Paris, and brings us, with an ironical and fitting grimness, to the threshold of the 1960's. It is because of this story, which is remarkable, and "Man of All Work," which is a masterpiece, that I cannot avoid feeling that Wright, as he died, was acquiring a new tone, and a less uncertain esthetic distance, and a new depth.

Shortly after we learned of Richard Wright's death, a Negro woman who was re-reading *Native Son* told me that it meant more to her now than it had when she had first read it. This, she said, was because the specific social climate which had produced it, or with which it was identified, seemed archaic now, was fading from our memories. Now, there was only the book itself to deal with, for it could no longer be read, as it had been read in 1940, as a militant racial manifesto. Today's racial manifestoes were being written very differently, and in many different languages; what mattered about the book now was how accurately or deeply the life of Chicago's South Side had been conveyed.

I think that my friend may prove to be right. Certainly, the two oldest stories in this book, "The Man Who Was Almost a Man," and "The Man Who Saw the Flood," both Depression stories, both occurring in the South, and both, of course, about Negroes, do not seem dated. Perhaps it is odd, but they did not make me think of the 1930's, or even, particularly, of Negroes. They made me think of human loss and helplessness. There is a dry, savage, folkloric humor in "The Man Who Was Almost a Man." It tells the story of a boy who wants a gun, finally manages to get one, and, by a hideous error, shoots a white man's mule. He then takes to

the rails, for he would have needed two years to pay
for the mule. There is nothing funny about "The Man
Who Saw the Flood," which is as spare and moving an
account as that delivered by Bessie Smith in "Back-
water Blues."

It is strange to begin to suspect, now, that Richard
Wright was never, really, the social and polemical writer
he took himself to be. In my own relations with him, I
was always exasperated by his notions of society, politics, and history, for they seemed to me utterly fanciful.
I never believed that he had any real sense of how a
society is put together. It had not occurred to me, and
perhaps it had not occurred to him, that his major interests as well as his power lay elsewhere. Or perhaps it
had occurred to me, for I distrusted his association with
the French intellectuals, Sartre, de Beauvoir, and company. I am not being vindictive toward them or condescending toward Richard Wright when I say that it
seemed to me that there was very little they could give
him which he could use. It has always seemed to me
that ideas were somewhat more real to them than people;
but anyway, and this is a statement made with the very
greatest love and respect, I always sensed in Richard
Wright a Mississippi pickaninny, mischievous, cunning,
and tough. This always seemed to be at the bottom of
everything he said and did, like some fantastic jewel
buried in high grass. And it was painful to feel that

the people of his adopted country were no more capable of seeing this jewel than were the people of his native land, and were in their own way as intimidated by it.

Even more painful was the suspicion that Wright did not want to know this. The meaning of Europe for an American Negro was one of the things about which Richard Wright and I disagreed most vehemently. He was fond of referring to Paris as the "city of refuge"— which it certainly was, God knows, for the likes of us. But it was not a city of refuge for the French, still less for anyone belonging to France; and it would not have been a city of refuge for us if we had not been armed with American passports. It did not seem worthwhile to me to have fled the native fantasy only to embrace a foreign one. (Someone, some day, should do a study in depth of the role of the American Negro in the mind and life of Europe, and the extraordinary perils, different from those of America but not less grave, which the American Negro encounters in the Old World.)

But now that the storm of Wright's life is over, and politics is ended forever for him, along with the Negro problem and the fearful conundrum of Africa, it seems to have been the tough and intuitive, the genuine Richard Wright, who was being recorded all along. It now begins to seem, for example, that Wright's unrelentingly bleak landscape was not merely that of the Deep South, or of Chicago, but that of the world, of the human heart.

The landscape does not change in any of these stories. Even the most good-natured performance this book contains, good-natured by comparison only, "Big Black Good Man," takes place in Copenhagen in the winter, and in the vastly more chilling confines of a Danish hotel-keeper's fears.

In "Man of All Work," a tight, raging, diamond-hard exercise in irony, a Negro male who cannot find a job dresses himself up in his wife's clothes and hires himself out as a cook. ("Who," he demands of his horrified, bedridden wife, "ever looks at us colored folks anyhow?") He gets the job, and Wright uses this incredible situation to reveal, with beautiful spite and accuracy, the private lives of the master race. The story is told entirely in dialogue, which perfectly accomplishes what it sets out to do, racing along like a locomotive and suggesting far more than it states.

The story, without seeming to, goes very deeply into the demoralization of the Negro male and the resulting fragmentization of the Negro family which occurs when the female is forced to play the male role of breadwinner. It is also a maliciously funny indictment of the sexual terror and hostility of American whites: and the horror of the story is increased by its humor.

"Man, God Ain't Like That," is a fable of an African's discovery of God. It is a far more horrible story than "Man of All Work," but it too manages its effects by a kind of Grand Guignol humor, and it too is an unsparing indictment of the frivolity, egotism, and wrong-headedness of white people—in this case, a French artist and his mistress. It too is told entirely in dialogue and recounts how a French artist traveling through Africa picks up an African servant, uses him as a model, and, in order to shock and titillate his jaded European friends, brings the African back to Paris with him.

Whether or not Wright's vision of the African sensibility will be recognized by Africans, I do not know. But certainly he has managed a frightening and truthful comment on the inexorably mysterious and dangerous relationships between ways of life, which are also ways of thought. This story and "Man of All Work" left me wondering how much richer our extremely poor theater might now be if Wright had chosen to work in it.

But "The Man Who Killed a Shadow" is something else again; it is Wright at the mercy of his subject. His great forte, it now seems to me, was an ability to convey inward states by means of externals: "The Man Who Lived Underground," for example, conveys the spiritual horror of a man and a city by a relentless accumulation of details, and by a series of brief, sharply cut-off tableaus, seen through chinks and cracks and keyholes. The specifically sexual horror faced by a Negro cannot be dealt with in this way. "The Man Who Killed a Shadow" is a story of rape and murder, and neither the murderer nor his victim ever comes alive. The entire story seems to be occurring, somehow, beneath cotton.

There are many reasons for this. In most of the novels
written by Negroes until today (with the exception of
Chester Hime's *If He Hollers Let Him Go*) there is a
great space where sex ought to be; and what usually
fills this space is violence.

This violence, as in so much of Wright's work, is
gratuitous and compulsive. It is one of the severest
criticisms than can be leveled against his work. The
violence is gratuitous and compulsive because the root
of the violence is never examined. The root is rage. It
is the rage, almost literally the howl, of a man who is
being castrated. I do not think that I am the first person
to notice this, but there is probably no greater (or more
misleading) body of sexual myths in the world today
than those which have proliferated around the figure of
the American Negro. This means that he is penalized
for the guilty imagination of the white people who in-
vest him with their hates and longings, and is the
principal target of their sexual paranoia. Thus, when
in Wright's pages a Negro male is found hacking a
white woman to death, the very gusto with which this
is done, and the great attention paid to the details of
physical destruction reveal a terrible attempt to break
out of the cage in which the American imagination has
imprisoned him for so long.

In the meantime, the man I fought so hard and who
meant so much to me, is gone. First America, then

Europe, then Africa failed him. He lived long enough
to find all of the terms on which he had been born become obsolete; presently, all of his attitudes seemed
to be historical. But as his life ended, he seems to me
to have been approaching a new beginning. He had
survived, as it were, his own obsolescence, and his
imagination was beginning to grapple with that darkest
of all dark strangers for him, the African. The depth
thus touched in him brought him a new power and a new
tone. He had survived exile on three continents and
lived long enough to begin to tell the tale.

II. The Exile

I WAS FAR FROM IMAGINING, when I agreed to write this memoir, that it would prove to be such a painful and difficult task. What, after all, can I really say about Richard . . . ? Everything founders in the sea of what might have been. We might have been friends, for example, but I cannot honestly say that we were. There might have been some way of avoiding our quarrel, our rupture; I can only say that I failed to find it. The quarrel having occurred, perhaps there might have been a way to have become reconciled. I think, in fact, that I counted on this coming about in some mysterious, irrevocable way, the way a child dreams of winning, by means of some dazzling exploit, the love of his parents.

However, he is dead now, and so we never shall be reconciled. The debt I owe him can now never be discharged, at least not in the way I hoped to be able to discharge it. In fact, the saddest thing about our relationship is that my only means of discharging my debt to Richard was to become a writer; and this effort revealed, more and more clearly as the years went on, the deep and irreconcilable differences between our points of view.

This might not have been so serious if I had been older when we met. . . . If I had been, that is, less uncertain of myself, and less monstrously egotistical. But when we met, I was twenty, a carnivorous age; he was then as old as I am now, thirty-six; he had been my idol since high school, and I, as the fledgling Negro writer, was very shortly in the position of his protégé. This position was not really fair to either of us. As writers we were about as unlike as any two writers could possibly be. But no one can read the future, and neither of us knew this then. We were linked together, really, because both of us were black. I had made my pilgrimage to meet him because he was the greatest black writer in the world for me. In *Uncle Tom's Children,* in *Native Son,* and, above all, in *Black Boy,* I found expressed, for the first time in my life, the sorrow, the rage, and the murderous bitterness which was eating up my life and the lives of those around me. His work was an immense liberation and revelation for me. He became my ally and my witness, and alas! my father.

I remember our first meeting very well. It was in Brooklyn; it was winter, I was broke, naturally, shabby, hungry, and scared. He appeared from the depths of what I remember as an extremely long apartment. Now his face, voice, manner, figure are all very sadly familiar to me. But they were a great shock to me then. It is always a shock to meet famous men. There is always an irreducible injustice in the encounter, for the famous man cannot possibly fit the image which one has evolved of him. My own image of Richard was almost certainly based on Canada Lee's terrifying stage portrait of Bigger Thomas. Richard was not like that at all. His voice was light and even rather sweet, with a Southern melody in it; his body was more round than square, more square than tall; and his grin was more boyish than I had expected, and more diffident. He had a trick, when he greeted me, of saying, "Hey, boy!" with a kind of pleased, surprised expression on his face. It was very friendly, and it was also, faintly, mockingly conspiratorial—as though we were two black boys, in league against the world, and had just managed to spirit away several loads of watermelon.

We sat in the living room and Richard brought out a bottle of bourbon and ice and glasses. Ellen Wright was somewhere in the back with the baby, and made only one brief appearance near the end of the evening. I did not drink in those days, did not know how to drink, and I was terrified that the liquor, on my empty stomach, would have the most disastrous consequences. Richard talked to me or, rather, drew me out on the subject of the novel I was working on then. I was so afraid of falling off my chair and so anxious for him to be interested in me, that I told him far more about the novel than I, in fact, knew about it, madly improvising, one jump ahead of the bourbon, on all the themes which cluttered up my mind. I am sure that Richard realized this, for he seemed to be amused by me. But I think he liked me. I know that I liked him, then, and later, and all the time. But I also know that, later on, he did not believe this.

He agreed, that night, to read the sixty or seventy pages I had done on my novel as soon as I could send them to him. I didn't dawdle, naturally, about getting the pages in the mail, and Richard commented very kindly and favorably on them, and his support helped me to win the Eugene F. Saxton Fellowship. He was very proud of me then, and I was puffed up with pleasure that he was proud, and was determined to make him prouder still.

But this was not to be, for, as so often happens, my first real triumph turned out to be the herald of my first real defeat. There is very little point, I think, in regretting anything, and yet I do, nevertheless, rather regret that Richard and I had not become friends by this time, for it might have made a great deal of difference. We might at least have caught a glimpse of the difference between my mind and his; and if we could have argued about it then, our quarrel might not have been so painful later. But we had not become friends mainly, indeed, I suppose, because of this very difference, and also because I really was too young to be his friend and adored him too much and was too afraid of him. And this meant that when my first wintry exposure to the publishing

world had resulted in the irreparable ruin—carried out
by me—of my first novel, I scarcely knew how to face
anyone, let alone Richard. I was too ashamed of myself and I was sure that he was ashamed of me, too. This
was utter foolishness on my part, for Richard knew far
more about first novels and fledgling novelists than that;
but I had been out for his approval. It simply had not
occurred to me in those days that anyone *could* approve
of me if I had tried for something and failed. The young
think that failure is the Siberian end of the line, banish-
ment from all the living, and tend to do what I then did
—which was to hide.

I, nevertheless, did see him a few days before he
went to Paris in 1946. It was a strange meeting, melancholy in the way a theater is melancholy when the run
of the play is ended and the cast and crew are about to
be dispersed. All the relationships so laboriously created
now no longer exist, seem never to have existed; and the
future looks gray and problematical indeed. Richard's
apartment—by this time, he lived in the Village, on
Charles Street—seemed rather like that, dismantled,
everything teetering on the edge of oblivion; people
rushing in and out, friends, as I supposed, but alas,
most of them were merely admirers; and Richard and I
seemed really to be at the end of *our* rope, for he had
done what he could for me, and it had not worked out,
and now he was going away. It seemed to me that he was
sailing into the most splendid of futures, for he was
going, of all places! to France, and he had been invited

there by the French government. But Richard did not seem, though he was jaunty, to be overjoyed. There was a striking sobriety in his face that day. He talked a great deal about a friend of his, who was in trouble with the U.S. Immigration authorities, and was about to be, or already had been, deported. Richard was not being deported, of course, he was traveling to a foreign country as an honored guest; and he was vain enough and young enough and vivid enough to find this very pleasing and exciting. Yet he knew a great deal about exile, all artists do, especially American artists, especially American Negro artists. He had endured already, liberals and literary critics to the contrary, a long exile in his own country. He must have wondered what the real thing would be like. And he must have wondered, too, what would be the unimaginable effect on his daughter, who could now be raised in a country which would not penalize her on account of her color.

And that day was very nearly the last time Richard and I spoke to each other without the later, terrible warfare. Two years later, I, too, quit America, never intending to return. The day I got to Paris, before I even checked in at a hotel, I was carried to the Deux Magots, where Richard sat, with the editors of *Zero* magazine, "Hey, boy!" he cried, looking more surprised and pleased and conspiratorial than ever, and younger and happier. I took this meeting as a good omen, and I could not possibly have been more wrong.

I later became rather closely associated with *Zero*

magazine, and wrote for them the essay called "Everybody's Protest Novel." On the day the magazine was published, and before I had seen it, I walked into the Brasserie Lipp. Richard was there, and he called me over. I will never forget that interview, but I doubt that I will ever be able to re-create it.

Richard accused me of having betrayed him, and not only him but all American Negroes by attacking the idea of protest literature. It simply had not occurred to me that the essay could be interpreted in that way. I was still in that stage when I imagined that whatever was clear to me had only to be pointed out to become immediately clear to everyone. I was young enough to be proud of the essay and, sad and incomprehensible as it now sounds, I really think that I had rather expected to be patted on the head for my original point of view. It had not occurred to me that this point of view, which I had come to, after all, with some effort and some pain, could be looked on as treacherous or subversive. Again, I had mentioned Richard's *Native Son* at the end of the essay because it was the most important and most celebrated novel of Negro life to have appeared in America. Richard thought that I had attacked it, whereas, as far as I was concerned, I had scarcely even criticized it. And Richard thought that I was trying to destroy his novel and his reputation; but it had not entered my mind that either of these *could* be destroyed, and certainly not by me. And yet, what made the interview so ghastly was

not merely the foregoing or the fact that I could find no
words with which to defend myself. What made it most
painful was that Richard was right to be hurt, I was
wrong to have hurt him. He saw clearly enough, far
more clearly than I had dared to allow myself to see,
what I had done: I had used his work as a kind of spring-
board into my own. His work was a road-block in my
road, the sphinx, really, whose riddles I had to answer
before I could become myself. I thought confusedly then,
and feel very definitely now, that this was the greatest
tribute I could have paid him. But it is not an easy
tribute to bear and I do not know how I will take it
when my time comes. For, finally, Richard was hurt because I had not given him credit for any human feelings
or failings. And indeed I had not, he had never really
been a human being for me, he had been an idol. And
idols are created in order to be destroyed.

This quarrel was never really patched up, though it
must be said that, over a period of years, we tried.
"What do you mean, *protest!*" Richard cried. "*All*
literature is protest. You can't name a single novel that
isn't protest." To this I could only weakly counter that
all literature might be protest but all protest was not
literature. "Oh," he would say then, looking, as he so
often did, bewilderingly juvenile, "here you come again
with all that art for art's sake crap." This never failed
to make me furious, and my anger, for some reason,
always seemed to amuse him. Our rare, best times came

when we managed to exasperate each other to the point of helpless hilarity. "Roots," Richard would snort, when I had finally worked my way around to this dreary subject, "what——roots! Next thing you'll be telling me is that all colored folks have rhythm." Once, one evening, we managed to throw the whole terrifying subject to the winds, and Richard, Chester Himes, and myself went out and got drunk. It was a good night, perhaps the best I remember in all the time I knew Richard. For he and Chester were friends, they brought out the best in each other, and the atmosphere they created brought out the best in me. Three absolutely tense, unrelentingly egotistical, and driven people, free in Paris but far from home, with so much to be said and so little time in which to say it!

And time was flying. Part of the trouble between Richard and myself, after all, was that I was nearly twenty years younger and had never seen the South. Perhaps I can now imagine Richard's odyssey better than I could then, but it is only imagination. I have not, in my own flesh, traveled, and paid the price of such a journey, from the Deep South to Chicago to New York to Paris; and the world which produced Richard Wright has vanished and will never be seen again. Now, it seems almost in the twinkling of an eye, nearly twenty years have passed since Richard and I sat nervously over bourbon in his Brooklyn living room. These years have seen nearly all of the props of the Western reality knocked

out from under it, all of the world's capitals have
changed, the Deep South has changed, and Africa has
changed.

For a long time, it seems to me, Richard was cruelly
caught in this high wind. His ears, I think, were nearly
deafened by the roar, all about him, not only of falling
idols but of falling enemies. Strange people indeed
crossed oceans, from Africa and America, to come to
his door; and he really did not know who these people
were, and they very quickly sensed this. Not until the
very end of his life, judging by some of the stories in his
last book, *Eight Men*, did his imagination really begin
to assess the century's new and terrible dark stranger.
Well, he worked up until the end, died, as I hope to do,
in the middle of a sentence, and his work is now an
irreducible part of the history of our swift and terrible
time. Whoever He may be, and wherever you may be,
may God be with you, Richard, and may He help me
not to fail that argument which you began in me.

III. Alas, Poor Richard

AND MY RECORD'S CLEAR TODAY, the church brothers and sisters used to sing, *for He washed my sins away, And that old account was settled long ago!* Well, so, perhaps it was, for them; they were under the illusion that they could read their records right. I am far from certain that I am able to read my own record at all, I would certainly hesitate to say that I am able to read it right. And, as for accounts, it is doubtful that I have ever really "settled" an account in my life.

Not that I haven't tried. In my relations with Richard, I was always trying to set the record "straight," to "settle" the account. This is but another way of saying that I wanted Richard to see me, not as the youth I had been when he met me, but as a man. I wanted to feel that he had accepted me, had accepted my right to my own vision, my right, as his equal, to disagree with him. I nourished for a long time the illusion that this day was coming. One day, Richard would turn to me, with the light of sudden understanding on his face, and say, "Oh, *that's* what you mean." And then, so ran the dream, a great and invaluable dialogue would have begun. And the great value of this dialogue would have been not only in its power to instruct all of you, and the ages. Its great value would have been in its power to instruct me, its power to instruct Richard: for it would have been nothing less than that so universally desired, so rarely achieved reconciliation between spiritual father and spiritual son.

Now, of course, it is not Richard's fault that I felt this way. But there is not much point, on the other hand, in dismissing it as simply my fault, or my illusion. I had identified myself with him long before we met: in a sense by no means metaphysical, his example had helped me to survive. He was black, he was young, he had come out of the Mississippi nightmare and the Chicago slums, and he was a writer. He proved it could be done—proved it to me, and gave me an arm against all those others who assured me it could *not* be done. And I think I had expected Richard, on the day we met, somehow, miraculously, to understand this, and to rejoice in it. Perhaps that sounds foolish, but I cannot honestly say, not even now, that I really think it is foolish. Richard Wright had a tremendous effect on countless numbers of people whom he never met, multitudes whom he now will never meet. This means that his responsibilities and his hazards were great. I don't think that Richard ever thought of me as one of his responsibilities—*bien au contraire!*—but he certainly seemed, often enough, to wonder just what he had done to deserve me.

Our reconciliation, anyway, never took place. This

was a great loss for me. But many of our losses have a compensating gain. In my efforts to get through to Richard, I was forced to begin to wonder exactly why he held himself so rigidly against me. I could not believe—especially if one grants *my* reading of our relationship —that it could be due only to my criticism of his work. It seemed to me then, and it seems to me now, that one really needs those few people who take oneself and one's work seriously enough to be unimpressed by the public hullabaloo surrounding the former or the uncritical solemnity which menaces the latter from the instant that, for whatever reason, it finds itself in vogue.

No, it had to be more than that—the more especially as his attitude toward me had not, it turned out, been evolved for my particular benefit. It seemed to apply, with equal rigor, against a great many others. It applied against old friends, incontestably his equals, who had offended him, always, it turned out, in the same way: by failing to take his word for all the things he imagined, or had been led to believe, his word could cover. It applied against younger American Negroes who felt that Joyce, for example, not he, was the master; and also against younger American Negroes who felt that Richard did not know anything about jazz, or who insisted that the Mississippi and the Chicago he remembered were not precisely the Mississippi and the Chicago that they knew. It applied against Africans who refused to take Richard's word for Africa, and it applied against

Algerians who did not feel that Paris was all that Richard had it cracked up to be. It applied, in short, against anyone who seemed to threaten Richard's system of reality. As time went on, it seemed to me that these people became more numerous and that Richard had fewer and fewer friends. At least, most of those people whom I had known to be friends of Richard's seemed to be saddened by him, and, reluctantly, to drift away. He's been away too long, some of them said. He's cut himself off from his roots. I resisted this judgment with all my might, more for my own sake than for Richard's, for it was far too easy to find this judgment used against myself. For the same reason I defended Richard when an African told me, with a small, mocking laugh, *I believe he thinks he's white.* I did *not* think I had been away too long: but I could not fail to begin, however unwillingly, to wonder about the uses and hazards of expatriation. I did not think I was white, either, or I did not *think* I thought so. But the Africans might think I did, and who could blame them? In their eyes, and in terms of my history, I could scarcely be considered the purest or most dependable of black men.

And I think that it was at about this point that I began to watch Richard as though he were a kind of object lesson. I could not help wondering if he, when facing an African, felt the same awful tension between envy and despair, attraction and revulsion. I had always been considered very dark, both Negroes and whites had de-

spised me for it, and I had despised myself. But the
Africans were much darker than I; I was a paleface
among them, and so was Richard. And the disturbance
thus created caused all of my extreme ambivalence
about color to come floating to the surface of my mind.
The Africans seemed at once simpler and more devious,
more directly erotic and at the same time more subtle,
and they were proud. If they had ever despised themselves for their color, it did not show, as far as I could
tell. I envied them and feared them—feared that they
had good reason to despise me. What did Richard feel?
And what did Richard feel about other American Negroes abroad?

For example: one of my dearest friends, a Negro
writer now living in Spain, circled around me and I
around him for months before we spoke. One Negro
meeting another at an all-white cocktail party, or at that
larger cocktail party which is the American colony in
Europe, cannot but wonder how the other got there. The
question is: Is he for real? or is he kissing ass? Almost
all Negroes, as Richard once pointed out, are almost
always acting, but before a white audience—which is
quite incapable of judging their performance: and even
a "bad nigger" is, inevitably, giving something of a
performance, even if the entire purpose of his performance is to terrify or blackmail white people.

Negroes know about each other what can here be
called family secrets, and this means that one Negro, if

he wishes, can "knock" the other's "hustle"—can give
his game away. It is still not possible to overstate the
price a Negro pays to climb out of obscurity—for it is a
particular price, involved with being a Negro; and the
great wounds, gouges, amputations, losses, scars, endured in such a journey cannot be calculated. But even
this is not the worst of it, since he is really dealing with
two hierarchies, one white and one black, the latter
modeled on the former. The higher he rises, the less is
his journey worth, since (unless he is extremely energetic and anarchic, a genuinely "bad nigger" in the
most positive sense of the term) all he can possibly find
himself exposed to is the grim emptiness of the white
world—which does not live by the standards it uses to
victimize him—and the even more ghastly emptiness of
black people who wish they were white. Therefore, one
"exceptional" Negro watches another "exceptional"
Negro in order to find out if he knows how vastly suc-
cessful and bitterly funny the hoax has been. Alliances,
in the great cocktail party of the white man's world, are
formed, almost purely, on this basis, for if both of you
can laugh, you have a lot to laugh about. On the other
hand, if only one of you can laugh, one of you, inevitably, is laughing at the other.

In the case of my new-found friend, Andy, and I, we
were able, luckily, to laugh together. We were both
baffled by Richard, but still respectful and fond of him
—we accepted from Richard pronouncements and atti-

tudes which we would certainly never have accepted
from each other, or from anyone else—at the time Richard returned from wherever he had been to film *Native
Son*. (In which, to our horror, later abundantly justified,
he himself played Bigger Thomas.) He returned with a
brainstorm, which he outlined to me one bright, sunny
afternoon, on the terrace of the Royal St. Germain. He
wanted to do something to protect the rights of American Negroes in Paris; to form, in effect, a kind of pressure group which would force American businesses in
Paris, and American government offices, to hire Negroes
on a proportional basis.

This seemed unrealistic to me. How, I asked him, in
the first place, could one find out how many American
Negroes there were in Paris? Richard quoted an approximate, semi-official figure, which I do not remember, but I was still not satisfied. Of this number, how
many were looking for jobs? Richard seemed to feel
that they spent most of their time being turned down by
American bigots, but this was not really my impression.
I am not sure I said this, though, for Richard often made
me feel that the word "frivolous" had been coined to describe me. Nevertheless, my objections made him more
and more impatient with me, and I began to wonder if I
were not guilty of great disloyalty and indifference concerning the lot of American Negroes abroad. (I find that
there is something helplessly sardonic in my tone now,
as I write this, which also handicapped me on that dis-

tant afternoon. Richard, more than anyone I have ever known, brought this tendency to the fore in me. I always wanted to kick him, and say, "Oh, come off it, baby, ain't no white folks around now, let's tell it like it *is*.")

Still, most of the Negroes I knew had *not* come to Paris to look for work. They were writers or dancers or composers, they were on the G.I. Bill, or fellowships, or more mysterious shoestrings, or they worked as jazz musicians. I did not know anyone who doubted that the American hiring system remained in Paris exactly what it had been at home—but how was one to prove this, with a handful, at best, of problematical Negroes, scattered throughout Paris? Unlike Richard, I had no reason to suppose that any of them even *wanted* to work for Americans—my evidence, in fact, suggested that this was just about the last thing they wanted to do. But, even if they did, and even if they were qualified, how could one *prove* that So-and-So had not been hired by TWA *because* he was a Negro? I had found this almost impossible to do at home. Isn't this, I suggested, the kind of thing which ought to be done from Washington? Richard, however, was not to be put off, and he had made me feel so guilty that I agreed to find out how many Negroes were then working for the ECA.

There turned out to be two or three or four, I forget how many. In any case, we were dead, there being no way on earth to prove that there should have been six or seven. But we were all in too deep to be able to turn back now, and, accordingly, there was a pilot meeting of this extraordinary organization, quite late, as I remember, one evening, in a private room over a bistro. It was in some extremely inconvenient part of town, and we all arrived separately or by twos. (There was some vague notion, I think, of defeating the ever-present agents of the CIA, who certainly ought to have had better things to do, but who, quite probably, on the other hand, didn't.) We may have defeated pursuit on our way there, but there was certainly no way of defeating detection as we arrived: slinking casually past the gaping mouths and astounded eyes of a workingman's bistro, like a disorganized parade, some thirty or forty of us, through a back door, and up the stairs. My friend and I arrived a little late, perhaps a little drunk, and certainly on a laughing jag, for we felt that we had been trapped in one of the most improbable and old-fashioned of English melodramas.

But Richard was in his glory. He was on the platform above us, I think he was alone there; there were only Negroes in the room. The results of the investigations of others had proved no more conclusive than my own— one could certainly not, on the basis of our findings, attack a policy or evolve a strategy—but this did not seem to surprise Richard or, even, to disturb him. It was decided, since we could not be a pressure group, to form a fellowship club, the purpose of which would be to get to know the French, and help the French to get to know us. Given our temperaments, neither Andy nor myself felt any need to join a club for this, we were getting along just fine on our own; but, somewhat to my surprise, we did not know many of the other people in the room, and so we listened. If it were only going to be a social club, then, obviously, the problem, as far as we were concerned, was over.

Richard's speech, that evening, made a great impact on me. It frightened me. I felt, but suppressed the feeling, that he was being mightily condescending toward the people in the room. I suppressed the feeling because most of them did not, in fact, interest me very much; but I was still in that stage when I felt guilty about not loving every Negro that I met. Still, perhaps for this very reason, I could not help resenting Richard's aspect and Richard's tone. I do not remember how his speech began, but I will never forget how it ended. News of this get-together, he told us, had caused a great stir in Parisian intellectual circles. Everyone was filled with wonder (as well they might be) concerning the future of such a group. A great many white people had wished to be present, Sartre, de Beauvoir, Camus—"and," said Richard, *my own wife.* But I told them, before I can allow you to come, we've got to prepare the Negroes to receive you!"

This revelation, which was uttered with a smile, produced the most strained, stunned, uneasy silence. I looked at Andy, and Andy looked at me. There was something terribly funny about it, and there was something not funny at all. I rather wondered what the probable response would have been had Richard dared make such a statement in, say, a Negro barber shop; rather wondered, in fact, what the probable response would have been had anyone else dared make such a statement to anyone in the room, under different circumstances. ("Nigger, I been receiving white folks all my life—prepare *who?* Who you think you going to *prepare?*") It seemed to me, in any case, that the preparation ought, at least, to be conceived of as mutual: there was no reason to suppose that Parisian intellectuals were more "prepared" to "receive" American Negroes than American Negroes were to receive them—rather, all things considered, the contrary.

This was the extent of my connection with the Franco-American Fellowship Club, though the club itself, rather anemicly, seemed to drag on for some time. I do not know what it accomplished—very little, I should imagine; but it soon ceased to exist because it had never had any reason to come into existence. To judge from complaints I heard, Richard's interest in it, once it was —roughly speaking—launched, was minimal. He told me once that it had cost him a great deal of money—this referred, I think, to some disastrous project, involving a printer's bill, which the club had undertaken. It seemed, indeed, that Richard felt that, with the establishment of this club, he had paid his dues to American Negroes abroad, and at home, and forever; had paid his dues, and was off the hook, since they had once more proved themselves incapable of following where he led. For yet one or two years to come, young Negroes would cross the ocean and come to Richard's door, wanting his sympathy, his help, his time, his money. God knows it must have been trying. And yet, they could not possibly have taken up more of his time than did the dreary sycophants by whom, as far as I could tell, he was more and more surrounded. Richard and I, of course, drifted farther and farther apart—our dialogues became too frustrating and too acrid—but, from my helplessly sardonic distance, I could only make out, looming above what seemed to be an indescribably cacophonous parade of mediocrities, and a couple of the world's most empty and pompous black writers, the tough and loyal figure of Chester Himes. There was a noticeable chill in the love affair which had been going on between Richard and the French intellectuals. He had always made American intellectuals uneasy, and now they were relieved to discover that he bored them, and even more relieved to say so. By this time he had managed to estrange himself from almost all of the younger American Negro writers in Paris. They were often to be found in the same café, Richard compulsively playing the pin-ball machine, while they, spitefully and deliberately, refused to acknowledge his presence. Gone were the days when he had only to enter a café to be greeted with the American

Negro equivalent of "*cher maître*" ("Hey, Richard, how
you making it, my man? Sit down and tell me something"), to be seated at a table, while all the bright faces
turned toward him. The brightest faces were now turned
from him, and among these faces were the faces of the
Africans and the Algerians. They did not trust him—
and their distrust was venomous because they felt that
he had promised them so much. When the African said
to me *I believe he thinks he's white*, he meant that Richard cared more about his safety and comfort than he
cared about the black condition. But it was to this condition, at least in part, that he owed his safety and comfort and power and fame. If one-tenth of the suffering
which obtained (and obtains) among Africans and Algerians in Paris had been occurring in Chicago, one
could not help feeling that Richard would have raised
the roof. He never ceased to raise the roof, in fact, as far
as the American color problem was concerned. But time
passes quickly. The American Negroes had discovered
that Richard did not really know much about the present dimensions and complexity of the Negro problem
here, and, profoundly, did not want to know. And one
of the reasons that he did not want to know was that his
real impulse toward American Negroes, individually,
was to despise them. They, therefore, dismissed his rage
and his public pronouncements as an unmanly reflex; as
for the Africans, at least the younger ones, they knew he
did not know them and did not want to know them, and

they despised *him*. It must have been extremely hard to bear, and it was certainly very frightening to watch. I could not help feeling: *Be careful. Time is passing for you, too, and this may be happening to you one day.*

For who has not hated his black brother? Simply *because* he is black, *because* he is brother. And who has not dreamed of violence? That fantastical violence which will drown in blood, wash away in blood, not only generation upon generation of horror, but which will also release one from the individual horror, carried everywhere in the heart. Which of us has overcome his past? And the past of a Negro is blood dripping down through leaves, gouged-out eyeballs, the sex torn from its socket and severed with a knife. But this past is not special to the Negro. This horror is also the past, and the everlasting potential, or temptation, of the human race. If we do not know this, it seems to me, we know nothing about ourselves, nothing about each other; to have accepted this is also to have found a source of strength—source of all our power. But one must first accept this paradox, with joy.

The American Negro has paid a hidden, terrible price for his slow climbing to the light; so that, for example, Richard was able, at last, to live in Paris exactly as he would have lived, had he been a white man, here, in America. This may seem desirable, but I wonder if it is. Richard paid the price such an illusion of safety demands. The price is a turning away from, an ignorance of, all of the powers of darkness. This sounds mystical, but it is not; it is a hidden fact. It is the failure of the moral imagination of Europe which has created the forces now determined to overthrow it. No European dreamed, during Europe's heyday, that they were sowing, in a dark continent, far away, the seeds of a whirlwind. It was not dreamed, during the Second World War, that Churchill's ringing words to the English were overheard by English slaves—who, now, coming in their thousands to the mainland, menace the English sleep. It is only now, in America, and it may easily be too late, that any of the anguish, to say nothing of the rage, with which the American Negro has lived so long begins, dimly, to trouble the public mind. The suspicion has been planted—and the principal effect, so far, here, has been panic—that perhaps the world is darker and therefore more real than we have allowed ourselves to believe.

Time brought Richard, as it has brought the American Negro, to an extraordinarily baffling and dangerous place. An American Negro, however deep his sympathies, or however bright his rage, ceases to be simply a black man when he faces a black man from Africa. When I say simply a black man, I do not mean that being a black man is simple, anywhere. But I am suggesting that one of the prices an American Negro pays—or can pay—for what is called his "acceptance" is a profound, almost ineradicable self-hatred. This corrupts every aspect of his living, he is never at peace again, he is out of touch with himself forever. And, when he faces an African, he is facing the unspeakably dark, guilty, erotic past which the Protestant fathers made him bury—for their peace of mind, and for their power—but which lives in his personality and haunts the universe yet. What an African, facing an American Negro sees, I really do not yet know; and it is too early to tell with what scars and complexes the African has come up from the fire. But the war in the breast between blackness and whiteness, which caused Richard such pain, need not be a war. It is a war which just as it denies both the heights and the depths of our natures, takes, and has taken, visibly and invisibly, as many white lives as black ones. And, as I see it, Richard was among the most illustrious victims of this war. This is why, it seems to me, he eventually found himself wandering in a no-man's land between the black world and the white. It is no longer important to be white—thank heaven—the white face is no longer invested with the power of this world; and it is devoutly to be hoped that it will soon no longer be important to be black. The experience of the American Negro, if it is ever faced and assessed, makes it possible to hope for such a reconciliation. The hope and the effect of this fusion in the breast of the American Negro is one of the few hopes we have of surviving the wilderness which lies before us now.

13. The Black Boy Looks at the White Boy

I walked and I walked
Till I wore out my shoes.
I can't walk so far, but
Yonder come the blues.
                              —Ma Rainey

I FIRST MET NORMAN MAILER about five years ago, in Paris, at the home of Jean Malaquais. Let me bring in at once the theme that will repeat itself over and over throughout this love letter: I was then (and I have not changed much) a very tight, tense, lean, abnormally ambitious, abnormally intelligent, and hungry black cat. It is important that I admit that, at the time I met Norman, I was extremely worried about my career; and a writer who is worried about his career is also fighting for his life. I was approaching the end of a love affair, and I was not taking it very well. Norman and I are alike in this, that we both tend to suspect others of putting us down, and we strike before we're struck. Only, our styles are very different: I am a black boy from the Harlem streets, and Norman is a middle-class Jew. I am not dragging my personal history

216

into this gratuitously, and I hope I do not need to say that no sneer is implied in the above description of Norman. But these are the facts and in my own relationship to Norman they are crucial facts.

Also, I have no right to talk about Norman without risking a distinctly chilling self-exposure. I take him very seriously, he is very dear to me. And I think I know something about his journey from my black boy's point of view because my own journey is not really so very different, and also because I have spent most of my life, after all, watching white people and outwitting them, so that I might survive. I think that I know something about the American masculinity which most men of my generation do not know because they have not been menaced by it in the way that I have been. It is still true, alas, that to be an American Negro male is also to be a kind of walking phallic symbol: which means that one pays, in one's own personality, for the sexual insecurity of others. The relationship, therefore, of a black boy to a white boy is a very complex thing.

There is a difference, though, between Norman and myself in that I think he still imagines that he has something to save, whereas I have never had anything to lose. Or, perhaps I ought to put it another way: the things that most white people imagine that they can salvage from the storm of life is really, in sum, their innocence. It was this commodity precisely which I had to get rid of at once, literally, on pain of death. I am afraid that most of the white people I have ever known impressed me as being in the grip of a weird nostalgia, dreaming of a vanished state of security and order, against which dream, unfailingly and unconsciously, they tested and very often lost their lives. It is a terrible thing to say, but I am afraid that for a very long time the troubles of white people failed to impress me as being real trouble. They put me in mind of children crying because the breast has been taken away. Time and love have modified my tough-boy lack of charity, but the attitude sketched above was my first attitude and I am sure that there is a great deal of it left.

To proceed: two lean cats, one white and one black, met in a French living room. I had heard of him, he had heard of me. And here we were, suddenly, circling around each other. We liked each other at once, but each was frightened that the other would pull rank. He could have pulled rank on me because he was more famous and had more money and also because he was white; but I could have pulled rank on him precisely because I was black and knew more about that periphery he so helplessly maligns in *The White Negro* than he could ever hope to know. Already, you see, we were trapped in our roles and our attitudes: the toughest kid on the block was meeting the toughest kid on the block. I think that both of us were pretty weary of this grueling and thankless role, I know that I am; but the roles that we construct are constructed because we feel that they will help us to survive and also, of course, because they fulfill something in our personalities; and one does not, therefore, cease playing a role simply because one has begun to understand it. All roles are dangerous. The world tends to trap and immobilize you in the role you play; and it is not always easy—in fact, it is always extremely hard—to maintain a kind of watchful, mocking distance between oneself as one appears to be and oneself as one actually is.

I think that Norman was working on *The Deer Park* at that time, or had just finished it, and Malaquais, who had translated *The Naked and the Dead* into French, did not like *The Deer Park*. I had not then read the book; if I had, I would have been astonished that Norman could have expected Malaquais to like it. What Norman was trying to do in *The Deer Park*, and quite apart, now, from whether or not he succeeded, could only—it seems to me—baffle and annoy a French intellectual who seemed to me essentially rationalistic. Norman has many qualities and faults, but I have never heard anyone accuse him of possessing this particular one. But Malaquais' opinion seemed to mean a great deal to him—this astonished me, too; and there was a running, good-natured but astringent argument between them, with Malaquais playing the role of the old lion and Norman playing the role of the powerful but clumsy cub. And, I must say, I think that each of them got a great deal of pleasure out of the other's performance. The night we met, we stayed up very late, and did a great deal of drinking and shouting. But beneath all the shouting and the posing and the mutual showing off, something very wonderful was happening. I was aware of a new and warm presence in my life, for I had met someone I wanted to know, who wanted to know me.

Norman and his wife, Adele, along with a Negro jazz musician friend, and myself, met fairly often during the few weeks that found us all in the same city. I think that Norman had come in from Spain, and he was shortly to return to the States; and it was not long after Norman's departure that I left Paris for Corsica. My memory of that time is both blurred and sharp, and, oddly enough, is principally of Norman—confident, boastful, exuberant, and loving—striding through the soft Paris nights like a gladiator. And I think, alas, that I envied him: his success, and his youth, and his love. And this meant that though Norman really wanted to know me, and though I really wanted to know him, I hung back, held fire, danced, and lied. I was not going to come crawling out of my ruined house, all bloody, no, baby, sing no sad songs for *me*. And the great gap between Norman's state and my own had a terrible effect on our relationship, for it inevitably connected, not to say collided, with that myth of the sexuality of Negroes which Norman, like so many others, refuses to give up. The sexual battleground, if I may call it that, is really the same for everyone; and I, at this point, was just about to be carried off the battleground on my shield, if anyone could find it; so how could I play, in any way whatever, the noble savage?

At the same time, my temperament and my experience in this country had led me to expect very little from most American whites, especially, horribly enough, my friends: so it did not seem worthwhile to challenge, in any real way, Norman's views of life on the periphery, or to put him down for them. I was weary, to tell the truth. I had tried, in the States, to convey something of what it felt like to be a Negro and no one had been able to listen: they wanted their romance. And, anyway, the really ghastly thing about trying to convey to a white man the reality of the Negro experience has nothing whatever to do with the fact of color, but has to do with this man's relationship to his own life. He will face in your life only what he is willing to face in his. Well, this means that one finds oneself tampering with the insides of a stranger, to no purpose, which one probably has no right to do, and I chickened out. And matters were not helped at all by the fact that the Negro jazz musicians, among whom we sometimes found ourselves, who really liked Norman, did not for an instant consider him as being even remotely "hip" and Norman did not know this and I could not tell him. He never broke through to them, at least not as far I know; and they were far too "hip," if that is the word I want, even to consider breaking through to him. They thought he was a real sweet ofay cat, but a little frantic.

But we were far more cheerful than anything I've said

might indicate and none of the above seemed to matter
very much at the time. Other things mattered, like
walking and talking and drinking and eating, and the
way Adele laughed, and the way Norman argued. He
argued like a young man, he argued to win: and while
I found him charming, he may have found me exasperating, for I kept moving back before that short, prod-
ding forefinger. I couldn't submit my arguments, or
my real questions, for I had too much to hide. Or so it
seemed to me then. I submit, though I may be wrong,
that I was then at the beginning of a terrifying adven-
ture, not too unlike the conundrum which seems to menace Norman now:

"I had done a few things and earned a few pence";
but the things I had written were behind me, could not
be written again, could not be repeated. I was also real-
izing that all that the world could give me as an artist, it
had, in effect, already given. In the years that stretched
before me, all that I could look forward to, in that way,
were a few more prizes, or a lot more, and a little more,
or a lot more money. And my private life had failed—
had failed, had failed. One of the reasons I had fought
so hard, after all, was to wrest from the world fame and
money and love. And here I was, at thirty-two, finding
my notoriety hard to bear, since its principal effect was
to make me more lonely; money, it turned out, was
exactly like sex, you thought of nothing else if you didn't
have it and thought of other things if you did; and love,

as far as I could see, was over. Love seemed to be over not merely because an affair was ending; it would have seemed to be over under any circumstances; for it was the dream of love which was ending. I was beginning to realize, most unwillingly, all the things love could not do. It could not make me over, for example. It could not undo the journey which had made of me such a strange man and brought me to such a strange place.

But at that time it seemed only too clear that love had gone out of the world, and not, as I had thought once, because I was poor and ugly and obscure, but precisely because I was no longer any of these things. What point, then, was there in working if the best I could hope for was the Nobel Prize? And *how*, indeed, would I be able to keep on working if I could never be released from the prison of my egocentricity? By what act could I escape this horror? For horror it was, let us make no mistake about that.

And, beneath all this, which simplified nothing, was that sense, that suspicion—which is the glory and torment of every writer—that what was happening to me might be turned to good account, that I was trembling on the edge of great revelations, was being prepared for a very long journey, and might now begin, having survived my apprenticeship (but had I survived it?), a great work. I might really become a great writer. But in order to do this I would have to sit down at the typewriter again, alone—I would have to accept my despair:

and I could not do it. It really does not help to be a strong-willed person or, anyway, I think it is a great error to misunderstand the nature of the will. In the most important areas of anybody's life, the will usually operates as a traitor. My own will was busily pointing out to me the most fantastically unreal alternatives to my pain, all of which I tried, all of which—luckily—failed. When, late in the evening or early in the morning, Norman and Adele returned to their hotel on the Quai Voltaire, I wandered through Paris, the underside of Paris, drinking, screwing, fighting—it's a wonder I wasn't killed. And then it was morning, I would somehow be home—usually, anyway—and the typewriter would be there, staring at me; and the manuscript of the new novel, which it seemed I would never be able to achieve, and from which clearly I was never going to be released, was scattered all over the floor.

That's the way it is. I think it is the most dangerous point in the life of any artist, his longest, most hideous turning; and especially for a man, an American man, whose principle is action and whose jewel is optimism, who must now accept what certainly then seems to be a gray passivity and an endless despair. It is the point at which many artists lose their minds, or commit suicide, or throw themselves into good works, or try to enter politics. For all of this is happening not only in the wilderness of the soul, but in the real world which accomplishes its seductions not by offering you opportunities to be wicked but by offering opportunities to be good, to be active and effective, to be admired and central and apparently loved.

Norman came on to America, and I went to Corsica. We wrote each other a few times. I confided to Norman that I was very apprehensive about the reception of *Giovanni's Room,* and he was good enough to write some very encouraging things about it when it came out. The critics had jumped on him with both their left feet when he published *The Deer Park*—which I still had not read—and this created a kind of bond, or strengthened the bond already existing between us. About a year and several overflowing wastebaskets later, I, too, returned to America, not vastly improved by having been out of it, but not knowing where else to go; and one day, while I was sitting dully in my house, Norman called me from Connecticut. A few people were going to be there—for the weekend—and he wanted me to come, too. We had not seen each other since Paris.

Well, I wanted to go, that is, I wanted to see Norman; but I did not want to see any people, and so the tone of my acceptance was not very enthusiastic. I realized that he felt this, but I did not know what to do about it. He gave me train schedules and hung up.

Getting to Connecticut would have been no hassle if I could have pulled myself together to get to the train. And I was sorry, as I meandered around my house and

time flew and trains left, that I had not been more honest
with Norman and told him exactly how I felt. But I had
not known how to do this, or it had not really occurred
to me to do it, especially not over the phone.

So there was another phone call, I forget who called
whom, which went something like this:

N: Don't feel you have to. I'm not trying to bug you.

J: It's not that. It's just—

N: You don't really want to come, do you?

J: I don't really feel up to it.

N: I understand. I guess you just don't like the Connecticut gentry.

J: Well—don't you ever come to the city?

N: Sure. We'll see each other.

J: I hope so. I'd like to see you.

N: Okay, till then.

And he hung up. I thought, I ought to write him a
letter, but of course I did nothing of the sort. It was
around this time I went South, I think; anyway, we did
not see each other for a long time.

But I thought about him a great deal. The grapevine
keeps all of us advised of the others' movements, so I
knew when Norman left Connecticut for New York,
heard that he had been present at this or that party and
what he had said: usually something rude, often something penetrating, sometimes something so hilariously
silly that it was difficult to believe he had been serious.
(This was my reaction when I first heard his famous

running-for-President remark. I dismissed it. I was wrong.) Or he had been seen in this or that Village spot, in which unfailingly there would be someone—out of spite, idleness, envy, exasperation, out of the bottomless, eerie, aimless hostility which characterizes almost every bar in New York, to speak only of bars—to put him down. I heard of a couple of fist-fights, and, of course, I was always encountering people who hated his guts. These people always mildly surprised me, and so did the news of his fights: it was hard for me to imagine that anyone could really dislike Norman, anyone, that is, who had encountered him personally. I knew of one fight he had had, forced on him, apparently, by a blow-hard Village type whom I considered rather pathetic. I didn't blame Norman for this fight, but I couldn't help wondering why he bothered to rise to such a shapeless challenge. It seemed simpler, as I was always telling myself, just to stay out of Village bars.

And people talked about Norman with a kind of avid glee, which I found very ugly. Pleasure made their saliva flow, they sprayed and all but drooled, and their eyes shone with that blood-lust which is the only real tribute the mediocre are capable of bringing to the extraordinary. Many of the people who claimed to be seeing Norman all the time impressed me as being, to tell the truth, pitifully far beneath him. But this is also true, alas, of much of my own entourage. The people who are in one's life or merely continually in one's presence reveal a great deal about one's needs and terrors. Also, one's hopes.

I was not, however, on the scene. I was on the road— not quite, I trust, in the sense that Kerouac's boys are; but I presented, certainly, a moving target. And I was reading Norman Mailer. Before I had met him, I had only read *The Naked and The Dead*, *The White Negro*, and *Barbary Shore*—I think this is right, though it may be that I only read *The White Negro* later and confuse my reading of that piece with some of my discussions with Norman. Anyway, I could not, with the best will in the world, make any sense out of *The White Negro* and, in fact, it was hard for me to imagine that this essay had been written by the same man who wrote the novels. Both *The Naked and The Dead* and (for the most part) *Barbary Shore* are written in a lean, spare, muscular prose which accomplishes almost exactly what it sets out to do. Even *Barbary Shore*, which loses itself in its last half (and which deserves, by the way, far more serious treatment than it has received) never becomes as downright impenetrable as *The White Negro* does.

Now, much of this, I told myself, had to do with my resistance to the title, and with a kind of fury that so antique a vision of the blacks should, at this late hour, and in so many borrowed heirlooms, be stepping off the A train. But I was also baffled by the passion with which Norman appeared to be imitating so many people inferior to himself, i.e., Kerouac, and all the other Suzuki rhythm boys. From them, indeed, I expected nothing more than their pablum-clogged cries of *Kicks!* and *Holy!* It seemed very clear to me that their glorification of the orgasm was but a way of avoiding all of the terrors of life and love. But Norman knew better, had to know better. *The Naked and The Dead, Barbary Shore,* and *The Deer Park* proved it. In each of these novels, there is a toughness and subtlety of conception, and a sense of the danger and complexity of human relationships which one will search for in vain, not only in the work produced by the aforementioned coterie, but in most of the novels produced by Norman's contemporaries. What in the world, then, was he doing, slumming so outrageously, in such a dreary crowd?

For, exactly because he knew better, and in exactly the same way that no one can become more lewdly vicious than an imitation libertine, Norman felt compelled to carry their *mystique* further than they had, to be more "hip," or more "beat," to dominate, in fact, their dreaming field; and since this *mystique* depended on a total rejection of life, and insisted on the fulfillment of an infantile dream of love, the *mystique* could only be extended into violence. No one is more dangerous than he who imagines himself pure in heart: for his purity, by definition, is unassailable.

But *why* should it be necessary to borrow the Depression language of deprived Negroes, which eventually evolved into jive and bop talk, in order to justify such a

grim system of delusions? Why malign the sorely menaced sexuality of Negroes in order to justify the white
man's own sexual panic? Especially as, in Norman's
case, and as indicated by his work, he has a very real
sense of sexual responsibility, and, even, odd as it may
sound to some, of sexual morality, and a genuine com-
mitment to life. None of his people, I beg you to notice,
spend their lives on the road. They really become entangled with each other, and with life. They really suffer,
they spill real blood, they have real lives to lose. This
is no small achievement; in fact, it is absolutely rare.
No matter how uneven one judges Norman's work to be,
all of it is genuine work. No matter how harshly one
judges it, it is the work of a genuine novelist, and an
absolutely first-rate talent.

Which makes the questions I have tried to raise—or,
rather, the questions which Norman Mailer irresistibly
represents—all the more troubling and terrible. I certainly do not know the answers, and even if I did, this is
probably not the place to state them.

But I have a few ideas. Here is Kerouac, ruminating
on what I take to be the loss of the garden of Eden:

> At lilac evening I walked with every muscle ach-
> ing among the lights of 27th and Welton in the
> Denver colored section, wishing I were a Negro,
> feeling that the best the white world had offered
> was not enough ecstasy for me, not enough life,
> joy, kicks, darkness, music, not enough night. I

wished I were a Denver Mexican, or even a poor overworked Jap, anything but what I so drearily was, a "white man" disillusioned. All my life I'd had white ambitions. . . . I passed the dark porches of Mexican and Negro homes; soft voices were there, occasionally the dusky knee of some mysterious sensuous gal; and dark faces of the men behind rose arbors. Little children sat like sages in ancient rocking chairs.

Now, this is absolute nonsense, of course, objectively considered, and offensive nonsense at that: I would hate to be in Kerouac's shoes if he should ever be mad enough to read this aloud from the stage of Harlem's Apollo Theater.

And yet there is real pain in it, and real loss, however thin; and it *is* thin, like soup too long diluted; thin because it does not refer to reality, but to a dream. Compare it, at random, with any old blues:

> Backwater blues done caused me
> To pack my things and go.
> 'Cause my house fell down
> And I can't live there no mo'.

"Man," said a Negro musician to me once, talking about Norman, "the only trouble with that cat is that he's white." This does not mean exactly what it says— or, rather, it *does* mean exactly what it says, and not what it might be taken to mean—and it is a very shrewd

observation. What my friend meant was that to become
a Negro man, let alone a Negro artist, one had to make
oneself up as one went along. This had to be done in the
not-at-all-metaphorical teeth of the world's determination to destroy you. The world had prepared no place
for you, and if the world had its way, no place would
ever exist. Now, this is true for everyone, but, in the case
of a Negro, this truth is absolutely naked: if he deludes
himself about it, he will die. This is not the way this
truth presents itself to white men, who believe the world
is theirs and who, albeit unconsciously, expect the
world to help them in the achievement of their identity.
But the world does not do this—for anyone; the world
is not interested in anyone's identity. And, therefore, the
anguish which can overtake a white man comes in the
middle of his life, when he must make the almost inconceivable effort to divest himself of everything he has
ever expected or believed, when he must take himself
apart and put himself together again, walking out of the
world, into limbo, or into what certainly looks like
limbo. This cannot yet happen to any Negro of Norman's age, for the reason that his delusions and defenses
are either absolutely impenetrable by this time, or he
has failed to survive them. "I want to know how power
works," Norman once said to me, "how it really works,
in detail." Well, I know how power works, it has worked
on me, and if I didn't know how power worked, I would
be dead. And it goes without saying, perhaps, that I

have simply never been able to afford myself any illusions concerning the manipulation of that power. My revenge, I decided very early, would be to achieve a power which outlasts kingdoms.

II

When I finally saw Norman again, I was beginning to suspect daylight at the end of my long tunnel, it was a summer day, I was on my way back to Paris, and I was very cheerful. We were at an afternoon party, Norman was standing in the kitchen, a drink in his hand, holding forth for the benefit of a small group of people. There seemed something different about him, it was the belligerence of his stance, and the really rather pontifical tone of his voice. I had only seen him, remember, in Malaquais' living room, which Malaquais indefatigably dominates, and on various terraces and in various dives in Paris. I do not mean that there was anything unfriendly about him. On the contrary, he was smiling and having a ball. And yet—he was leaning against the refrigerator, rather as though he had his back to the wall, ready to take on all comers.

Norman has a trick, at least with me, of watching, somewhat ironically, as you stand on the edge of the crowd around him, waiting for his attention. I suppose this ought to be exasperating, but in fact I find it rather endearing, because it is so transparent and because he gets such a bang out of being the center of attention. So do I, of course, at least some of the time.

We talked, bantered, a little tensely, made the usual, doomed effort to bring each other up to date on what we had been doing. I did not want to talk about my novel, which was only just beginning to seem to take shape, and, therefore, did not dare ask him if he were working on a novel. He seemed very pleased to see me, and I was pleased to see him, but I also had the feeling that he had made up his mind about me, adversely, in some way. It was as though he were saying, Okay, so now I know who *you* are, baby.

I was taking a boat in a few days, and I asked him to call me.

"Oh, no," he said, grinning, and thrusting that forefinger at me, "*you* call me."

"That's fair enough," I said, and I left the party and went on back to Paris. While I was out of the country, Norman published *Advertisements for Myself*, which presently crossed the ocean to the apartment of James Jones. Bill Styron was also in Paris at that time, and one evening the three of us sat in Jim's living room, reading aloud, in a kind of drunken, masochistic fascination, Norman's judgment of our personalities and our work. Actually, I came off best, I suppose; there was less about me, and it was less venomous. But the condescenion infuriated me; also, to tell the truth, my feelings were hurt. I felt that if that was the way Norman felt about me, he should have told me so. He had said that I was incapable of saying "F--- you" to the reader. My first temptation was to send him a cable-gram which would disabuse him of that notion, at least insofar as one reader was concerned. But then I thought, No, I would be cool about it, and fail to react as he so clearly wanted me to. Also, I must say, his judgment of myself seemed so wide of the mark and so childish that it was hard to stay angry. I wondered what in the world was going on in his mind. Did he really suppose that he had now become the builder and destroyer of reputations,

And of *my* reputation?

We met in the Actors' Studio one afternoon, after a performance of *The Deer Park*—which I deliberately arrived too late to see, since I really did not know how I was going to react to Norman, and didn't want to betray myself by clobbering his play. When the dis-cussion ended, I stood, again on the edge of the crowd around him, waiting. Over someone's shoulder, our eyes met, and Norman smiled.

"We've got something to talk about," I told him.

"I figured that," he said, smiling.

We went to a bar, and sat opposite each other. I was relieved to discover that I was not angry, not even (as far as I could tell) at the bottom of my heart. But, "Why did you write those things about me?"

"Well, I'll tell you about that," he said—Norman

has several accents, and I think this was his Texas one
—"I sort of figured you had it coming to you."

"Why?"

"Well, I think there's some truth in it."

"Well, if you felt that way, why didn't you ever say
so—to me?"

"Well, I figured if this was going to break up our
friendship, something else would come along to break
it up just as fast."

I couldn't disagree with that.

"You're the only one I kind of regret hitting so
hard," he said, with a grin. "I think I—probably—
wouldn't say it quite that way now."

With this, I had to be content. We sat for perhaps an
hour, talking of other things and, again, I was struck
by his stance: leaning on the table, shoulders hunched,
seeming, really, to roll like a boxer's, and his hands moving as though he were dealing with a sparring partner.
And we were talking of physical courage, and the necessity of never letting another guy get the better of you.

I laughed. "Norman, I can't go through the world
the way you do because I haven't got your shoulders."

He grinned, as though I were his pupil. "But you're
a pretty tough little mother, too," he said, and referred
to one of the grimmer of my Village misadventures, a
misadventure which certainly proved that I had a dangerously sharp tongue, but which didn't really prove
anything about my courage. Which, anyway, I had
long ago given up trying to prove.

I did not see Norman again until Provincetown, just after his celebrated brush with the police there, which resulted, according to Norman, in making the climate of Provincetown as "mellow as Jello." The climate didn't seem very different to me—dull natives, dull tourists, malevolent policemen; I certainly, in any case, would never have dreamed of testing Norman's sanguine conclusion. But we had a great time, lying around the beach, and driving about, and we began to be closer than we had been for a long time.

It was during this Provincetown visit that I realized, for the first time, during a long exchange Norman and I had, in a kitchen, at someone else's party, that Norman was really fascinated by the nature of political power. But, though he said so, I did not really believe that he was fascinated by it as a possibility for himself. He was then doing the great piece on the Democratic convention which was published in *Esquire*, and I put his fascination down to that. I tend not to worry about writers as long as they are working—which is not as romantic as it may sound—and he seemed quite happy with his wife, his family, himself. I declined, naturally, to rise at dawn, as he apparently often did, to go running or swimming or boxing, but Norman seemed to get a great charge out of these admirable pursuits and didn't put me down too hard for my comparative decadence.

He and Adele and the two children took me to the plane one afternoon, the tiny plane which shuttles from Provincetown to Boston. It was a great day, clear and

sunny, and that was the way I felt: for it seemed to me
that we had all, at last, re-established our old connection.

And then I heard that Norman was running for mayor,
which I dismissed as a joke and refused to believe until
it became hideously clear that it was not a joke at all. I
was furious. I thought, You son of a bitch, you're
copping out. You're one of the very few writers around
who might really become a great writer, who might help
to excavate the buried consciousness of this country,
and you want to settle for being the lousy mayor of
New York. *It's not your job.* And I don't at all mean
to suggest that writers are not responsible to and for—
in any case, always for—the social order. I don't, for
that matter, even mean to suggest that Norman would
have made a particularly bad Mayor, though I confess
that I simply cannot see him in this role. And there is
probably some truth in the suggestion, put forward by
Norman and others, that the shock value of having
such a man in such an office, or merely running for such
an office, would have had a salutary effect on the life
of this city—particularly, I must say, as relates to our
young people, who are certainly in desperate need of
adults who love them and take them seriously, and whom
they can respect. (Serious citizens may not respect Norman, but young people do, and do not respect the serious citizens; and their instincts are quite sound.)

But I do not feel that a writer's responsibility can be
discharged in this way. I do not think, if one is a writer,

that one escapes it by trying to become something else. One does *not* become something else: one becomes nothing. And what is crucial here is that the writer, however unwillingly, always, somewhere, knows this. There is no structure he can build strong enough to keep out this self-knowledge. What *has* happened, however, time and time again, is that the fantasy structure the writer builds in order to escape his central responsibility operates not as his fortress, but his prison, and he perishes within it. Or: the structure he has built becomes so stifling, so lonely, so false, and acquires such a violent and dangerous life of its own, that he can break out of it only by bringing the entire structure down. With a great crash, inevitably, and on his own head, and on the heads of those closest to him. It is like smashing the windows one second before one asphyxiates; it is like burning down the house in order, at last, to be free of it. And this, I think, really, to touch upon it lightly, is the key to the events at that monstrous, baffling, and so publicized party. Nearly everyone in the world—or nearly everyone, at least, in this extraordinary city—was there: policemen, Mafia types, the people whom we quaintly refer to as "beatniks," writers, actors, editors, politicians, and gossip columnists. It must be admitted that it was a considerable achievement to have brought so many unlikely types together under one roof; and, in spite of everything, I can't help wishing that I had been there to witness the mutual bewilderment. But the point is that no politician would have dreamed of giving such a party in order to launch his mayoralty campaign. Such an imaginative route is not usually an attribute of politicians. In addition, the price one pays for pursuing any profession, or calling, is an intimate knowledge of its ugly side. It is scarcely worth observing that political activity is often, to put it mildly, pungent, and I think that Norman, perhaps for the first time, really doubted his ability to deal with such a world, and blindly struck his way out of it. We do not, in this country now, have much taste for, or any real sense of, the extremes human beings can reach; time will improve us in this regard; but in the meantime the general fear of experience is one of the reasons that the American writer has so peculiarly difficult and dangerous a time.

One can never really see into the heart, the mind, the soul of another. Norman is my very good friend, but perhaps I do not really understand him at all, and perhaps everything I have tried to suggest in the foregoing is false. I do not think so, but it may be. One thing, however, I am certain is *not* false, and that is simply the fact of his being a writer, and the incalculable potential he as a writer contains. His work, after all, is all that will be left when the newspapers are yellowed, all the gossip columnists silenced, and all the cocktail parties over, and when Norman and you and I are dead. I know that this point of view is not terribly fashionable these days, but I think we *do* have a responsibility, not only to ourselves and to our own time, but to those who are coming after us. (I refuse to believe that no one is coming after us.) And I suppose that this responsibility can only be discharged by dealing as truthfully as we know how with our present fortunes, these present days. So that my concern with Norman, finally, has to do with how deeply he has understood these last sad and stormy events. If he has understood them, then he is richer and we are richer, too; if he has not understood them, we are all much poorer. For, though it clearly needs to be brought into focus, he has a real vision of ourselves as we are, and it cannot be too often repeated in this country now, that, where there is no vision, the people perish.

VINTAGE INTERNATIONAL

POSSESSION
by A. S. Byatt

An intellectual mystery and a triumphant love story of a pair of young scholars researching the lives of two Victorian poets.

"Gorgeously written . . . a tour de force." —*The New York Times Book Review*

Winner of the Booker Prize
Fiction/Literature/0-679-73590-9

THE REMAINS OF THE DAY
by Kazuo Ishiguro

A profoundly compelling portrait of the perfect English butler and of his fading, insular world in postwar England.

"One of the best books of the year." —*The New York Times Book Review*

Fiction/Literature/0-679-73172-5

ALL THE PRETTY HORSES
by Cormac McCarthy

At sixteen, John Grady Cole finds himself at the end of a long line of Texas ranchers, cut off from the only life he has ever imagined for himself. With two companions, he sets off for Mexico on a sometimes idyllic, sometimes comic journey, to a place where dreams are paid for in blood.

"A book of remarkable beauty and strength, the work of a master in perfect command of his medium." —*Washington Post Book World*

Winner of the National Book Award for Fiction
Fiction/Literature/0-679-74439-8

THE ENGLISH PATIENT
by Michael Ondaatje

During the final moments of World War II, four damaged people come together in a deserted Italian villa. As their stories unfold, a complex tapestry of image and emotion is woven, leaving them inextricably connected by the brutal circumstances of war.

"It seduces and beguiles us with its many-layered mysteries, its brilliantly taut and lyrical prose, its tender regard for its characters." —*Newsday*

Winner of the Booker Prize
Fiction/Literature/0-679-74520-3

VINTAGE INTERNATIONAL